To my dearest husband, Daniel, for always believing in me.

The Lost Huntress

The Farrowspire Chronicles, Volume 1

Samantha Brink

Published by Samantha Brink, 2023.

THE LOST HUNTRESS

First edition. December 6, 2023.

Copyright © 2023 Samantha Brink.

ISBN: 979-8223790457

Written by Samantha Brink.

Table of Contents

Chapter 1

An Unlikely Alliance

The view from Mount Feinberg was spectacular at this time of year. The mountain rose high and towered over the valley where the village of Melas lay nestled in its shadow. Many quaint cottages dotted the landscape, farms spread along the outskirts, and from so high up, it was as though the whole land bowed to the Feinberg. The warm evening showers from the last two weeks had thawed the many frozen streams and ponds that lay in the valley so that sunshine glittered off pools of water like millions of golden diamonds. Loud, shrill breezes whistled through the land where daffodils danced in the wind, but the tranquillity and beauty felt out of place. It was a trickery, hiding the evil that lived there as though trying to trap lonely travellers with its guile.

From halfway up the Feinberg, a small campsite could be found beside a shallow cave and lazy stream, overlooking the picturesque landscape - admiring the splendour while aware of its lies. The floor of the forested area was carpeted in brilliant purple with a canopy to match and bees buzzed, busily collecting pollen from the blossoms. The small tent that had been erected amidst the trees had already started to disappear into the surroundings, covered with the purple flowers made wet from the thunderstorm the night before. The beauty did not, however, make up for the slight chill the dampness caused, nor did it make the rumbles of thunder through the evening sky and the expectation of more rain any less unpleasant. The two men who occupied the campsite sat beside a small fire hidden from view by the overhanging rock, battling against the elements to keep it going.

Gavin Matterson was the larger of the two men. His head was balding and grey, and he had the appearance of a huge, hairy grizzly bear, with the personality of one, too. He had muscles to spare, making him perfect for the hunter's guild, the Shikari. When there was an important and difficult task that needed to be done, Gavin was the Shikari chosen; it was said he could kill the target with a flex of his forearm. His strength and viciousness were the reason he rose so quickly in the ranks to fill the role of one of the Shikari's top leaders. It was also why he had been chosen for this particular job that had the two men waiting on the mountain overlooking Melas, a job he was already beginning to resent after last night's storm and this night's imminent one. He sat in his leather armour, scowling at the fire while sharpening his dagger, and let out a grumble of discontent. The second man to his left shot him a bemused glance.

This man was the exact opposite of Gavin Matterson; where Gavin was extremely muscular, strong, and grumpy, Darwin Kimberley was skinny and tall, and as swift as a fox. He had a mop of sandy hair and small, shrewd eyes. He was also mischievous and his usual expression was one of amusement, though, currently, he was finding very little amusing. He found Gavin a particularly hilarious man, which was why he was the only Shikari who could be partnered with Gavin; while all the other hunters disliked Gavin's surly personality, Darwin was quite fond of his friend, knowing that, deep down, Gavin was not so much a grizzly bear as he was a teddy bear. Now, while Darwin couldn't say he was enjoying this mission so much as all the others they had been on together, he had felt a thrill of excitement during their mission briefing at the thought of who their targets were. He, too, wore leather armour and sat picking at their meagre meal of bread and ham. He glanced down past the trees into the valley below to marvel at how such beauty could surround a village of such darkness and evil.

They had arrived on this mountain two weeks prior, but they were not the only ones camping on the mountainside. They were, however, the only ones remaining hidden. Ten Shifters, two from each of the five Newid tribes, had soon joined the two men in their wait, one after the other. With so much activity on the Feinberg, more than it had seen in almost a century, both Gavin and Darwin had fully expected a fight to break out between the Newids, whose rivalry had always caused tension between the tribes.

The arrival of the Newids had initially surprised the two Shikari; Darwin and Gavin had fully expected to be camping alone on the mountain, yet, somehow, they, too, must have been informed of the prophecy. The birth of the child must be more important than their Master had let on, they had realised. Whether the Newids had also been told by the same spy within the village, or they had found out another way, mattered not; what was important was what they wished to do with the child should they get their hands on her first. But, even more imperative for Darwin and Gavin than anything else at this time of waiting was that they remained hidden from both the Enchantresses and Newids, especially the Enchantresses.

The Coven of the Dark, who resided in the valley, were not known to be the welcoming type. In fact, of the seven Enchantress families, the Enchantresses of the Coven of the Dark were the most feared and distrusted. They were usually ostracised by all who lived in Arantaea, and, it was said, by even those past the borders in the Baetalund and Vildahns of Mid-Eberra, though there weren't many who had ventured there and come back. Their practices had been called evil, and despicable, and the many fireplace stories told on Winter's Eve described the Enchantresses as hideously marked; the story went that they had been cursed for their deeds and this curse had left the Coven of the Dark scarred, forever identifiable by their distorted features.

A flash of lightning zigzagged through the evening sky, momentarily lighting the darkening mountain below. Darwin and

Gavin looked up warily. It was going to be another long and wet night. The only good thing so far was that having finally won the battle against the elements, Gavin and Darwin's fire crackled merrily, casting dancing lights and shadows around the inside of the small cave. All was calm and quiet when Gavin suddenly stilled and held up a hand in warning to Darwin. He put a finger to his lips and motioned to listen. They both sat for what felt like an age, Darwin straining his ears to hear what Gavin had heard. Just as he was starting to wonder if Gavin had imagined hearing something, a crash of thunder made them both jump.

"Did you hear that?" murmured Gavin, his deep voice louder than intended, echoing through the undergrowth and small cave. Frowning in concern, he stood up and turned slowly, holding his dagger ready.

"The thunder?" replied Darwin, bemused, though still alert. "A bit hard to miss, Gav."

"No, you dunce. Listen."

They remained silent for a few seconds.

Gavin raised his eyebrows at Darwin. "Surely you can hear it now?"

Darwin nodded. A soft rustling, almost indistinguishable from the rumbling of the thunderous sky, was drawing nearer. Darwin picked up the sheathed broad sword that lay beside him and moved to Gavin's side.

"What is it, do you think?" Darwin murmured, his brow pinched in concentration.

"Shh."

"Not the Enchantresses, I hope."

"I said quiet!"

The rustling stopped and between two tree trunks at the far end of their campsite, they could make out two eyes and canine features. The creature loped into the campsite, stopping a few feet away, its jowls lifted in a soft growl. ◈

"Just a wolf," sighed Gavin in slight disappointment, lowering his knife slightly.

The creature had golden eyes that shone in the firelight and it considered them carefully, as though assessing their worth as a meal. Its thick, grey fur stood on end along its back; it was a magnificent beast, fearfully strong and dangerous.

"What if it is one of them?" Darwin asked warily.

Gavin stilled as he considered this. "That wolf doesn't appear to have the markings of a shifter... but just to be sure...." Gavin flipped his dagger, aiming the hilt at the wolf. In an instant, he sent the dagger flying across the campsite. Had all been normal, the knife would have embedded itself in the wolf's side. But all was not normal; the knife cut through the air with deadly accuracy and hit an invisible wall with an echoing clang, then landed with a soft thud on the purple-blossomed ground.

Darwin's eyes widened while Gavin's narrowed, and both unsheathed their swords, but what they saw made them pause as, out of the shadows of the trees, stepped a woman whose outstretched hand glittered with power: an Enchantress. But this Enchantress was not at all what they'd expected. The stories they'd been told as children had them fully expecting to meet a tall, woman-like creature with hair like seaweed and skin like melting candle wax, eyes like depthless black pits, and claw-like nails. The only thing that had been true, it seemed, was her height. From the light of the fire, they could see she was gorgeous. She had long, dark, purple-black hair and eyes of a similar purplish hue, pale skin with a slight blush, and full, deep red, painted lips. She wore a long, silky black dress that seemed to flutter in its own breeze as she walked toward them to stand at the wolf's side. Her nails were long, but elegant and a deep red colour. Darwin and Gavin were gobsmacked, their mouths hanging slack.

"Close your mouths, humans," she said with a laugh, a beautiful, tinkling sound. She had a slight tilt to her voice, an accent that made her seem mysterious and alluring. Tossing her shimmering hair over her shoulders, she crossed her arms. Her laugh had not reached her eyes, which, Darwin had to admit, looked just as deadly as a viper's, coiled to strike. Both men shut their mouths with a pop, but did not put their weapons away: they knew better than to trust by beauty alone.

"I apologise for using magic," she continued, though not sounding sorry at all, "but I know how prone you humans are to killing things." The wolf growled again and the Enchantress rolled her eyes. "Please excuse Gundrel. He seems to think I need his protection."

The wolf glanced back at her with reproach, causing both men to come to the same realisation: this was no mere wolf after all. Before their eyes, the wolf's body seemed to shift and contort, like a puzzle being ripped apart, and the cracks of bone and ripping skin that filled the clearing caused Darwin and Gavin to flinch in distaste. In seconds, a Newid man stood before them, the fur that previously covered his body transformed into a grey tunic and pants. He glowered at the humans.

"I should rip you apart for your insolence in trying to kill me," he snarled at them. He spoke in a rough voice and his accent was indicative of the Lahntberg region. The Newid had long, silver hair and furry, pointed ears and was quite handsome in a rough and rugged way. He had golden eyes that took the two men in with a proudness and cautiousness. His nails also remained claw-like and even the way he held himself was still slightly animalistic.

The Enchantress clicked her fingers and black smoke drifted out of her fingertips, slowly changing form into solid material that draped itself over the Newid, covering him in a flowing black cloak, hiding the grey tunic and pants that would have previously stood out in the night. As it did so, he straightened and turned to them, looking almost human except for his ears and eyes. The Enchantress stepped forward past the Newid, raising her hands as Darwin and Gavin both readied their weapons.

"I wish for you to hear what I have to say, humans. I am Imogen and-"

"Why should we listen to anything an Enchantress of the Coven of the Dark has to say, let alone a Newid?" snapped Darwin, spitting on the ground, and Gundrel snarled in anger, showing two fang-like incisors.

"Shut up, Gundrel," Imogen said sharply, throwing him a dark look, before turning back to Darwin and Gavin. Her eyes seemed to glitter dangerously, and Darwin swallowed nervously. "You will hear what I have to say because I speak for my mistress, the same Enchantress who sent for you."

"The spy is an Enchantress?" Darwin blurted out in surprise, glancing at Gavin, who, he was not relieved to see, did not look as shocked and disbelieving as he felt. "I assumed she was one of us," he whispered sideways to Gavin.

Gavin glanced at Darwin, aghast. "A Shikari?" he whispered back, sharply. "Really, Dar, you thought a Shikari would be the spy?" He sighed and rolled his eyes, then turned back to the Enchantress and wolf-man. "I was unaware more of your kind were in on the plan and I was also under the impression only we were told." He looked pointedly at Gundrel.

"Just myself, my mistress, and Gundrel and his master, know of the plan aside from you two."

"And yet the forest is full of Newids."

Imogen sighed in frustration. "We do not have time for this. She has gone into labour."

Gavin frowned and looked ready to interrupt her, but Imogen held up her hand, pursing her lips. "There is no time," she repeated, growing impatient. "So far, we have managed to keep her going into labour a secret from the rest of the Newids and the Köning, our queen. If it will put your mind at ease, the other Newids are only here for the celebration that will be held tomorrow night."

Darwin, still struggling to come to terms with the new information, nodded his head in Gundrel's direction and said, "Why is he here?"

"I am here because the child is just as important to us," growled Gundrel.

Imogen sighed and said, "We must be going. Please." She stepped forward again. "Your Master said you would help us."

Darwin glanced at Gavin and was surprised to see him finally nod and lower his sword. "We will come, but you will answer our questions."

Imogen nodded and said, "Follow me, then."

Darwin grumbled to himself. He was not happy with this plan, but he did not dare say anything contrary to Gavin's decision in front of the wolf and Enchantress. He made his way with Gavin toward Gundrel and Imogen and followed them out of the campsite. It was dark, almost too dark to make out a path, but the occasional flashes of lightning that shot across the sky, forming web-like patterns, lit the floor of the mountain long enough, and enough times, that they were able to keep their footing. Even so, both men were finding it increasingly more difficult to keep up with Imogen and Gundrel, who were both walking too quickly, widening the gap between the two men.

The longer they walked, the closer the village began to appear and the view of it became clearer. Darwin looked down into the dark valley. The landscape was speckled with lights from the dozen or so cottages that had been built below. There was no indication that the occupants were at all bad, let alone dangerous. In fact, it looked picturesque, like stars had been painted across the valley to match the night sky, and the homes, with the smoke escaping the chimneys, looked inviting rather than terrifying. Darwin shook his head. The picture did not match the deeds that took place, especially with what would soon be born. He could not help the thrill of excitement that shot through him.

It took only several minutes of climbing, or occasionally tripping, over winding tree roots, jumping over crystal clear, trickling streams, and ducking under low-hanging branches before Darwin could contain himself no longer and, taking advantage of the distance that had grown between the two men and the wolf-man and Enchantress, he whispered to Gavin, "How can you be so sure we can trust her after hearing about the magic they used on the child? They're sick." He spat on the ground in disgust. He was answered by a sharp clout as Gavin hit him over the head, glancing hastily at the Newid and Enchantress, who, thankfully, had not seemed to have heard Darwin.

Darwin, noticing this, too, added casually, "I had hoped we'd get the chance to kill some Coven of the Dark. I hear you gain some of their power for a short while if you kill one of them."

Gavin stopped suddenly, grabbing Darwin by the arm and pushing his drawn dagger to his side. "You will do no such thing. You'd jeopardise the whole mission. 'Gain their power' - what utter rubbish. Do you listen to every old wives' tale you hear?"

"There's always some truth to those tales," Darwin replied, shrugging.

"Is everything okay?" said a musical voice suddenly. Lightning forked across the sky, showing that Imogen and Gundrel had stopped and were looking at the two men suspiciously. Then they were plunged back into almost darkness, a rumble of thunder answering the strike of lightning.

Hastily putting his dagger away, Gavin gave Darwin a stern look and whispered, "Shut up, and don't do anything you'll regret." Then he turned forward and replied, "Apologies."

"What do you two not understand by time being of the essence," snarled Gundrel, angrily.

"We must keep moving," said Imogen from the darkness. Her dark form turned without another word and started on swiftly again, pulling Gundrel after her. Darwin glanced at Gavin, who sighed and quickly followed after them. Darwin had no choice but to jog to catch up to the trio, accidentally walking into a tree with a loud thunk. He swore under his breath.

"Could you not magic a light for us," he finally whispered to her angrily once he'd caught up.

Lights suddenly flared into existence, tiny orbs similar to that of the fireflies, just enough to light up the area dimly, but not enough to draw attention. Darwin and Gavin blinked rapidly, getting used to the bright orbs, feeling as though they had bumped their heads and had sparks dancing across their vision. In the glow, they could make out Gundrel, who had obviously started to walk back to them in his frustration, looking down at the hand that Imogen had placed on his shoulder, stopping him in his tracks.

Imogen sneered slightly, saying, "Sorry, I forgot you humans don't have dark-vision."

The trek became a lot easier after that, though, even with the lights, the path remained difficult and both Darwin and Gavin struggled to keep up with the agile Newid and graceful Enchantress. Silence followed and for a while, all that could be heard was their soft footfalls and the rumbles of thunder. It had begun to drizzle and a fine mist slowly crept down the hill like a lion sneaking up on its prey.

Gavin finally broke the silence, asking, "Why are you helping your mistress?"

For a while, it seemed Imogen would not answer, until-

"In short, I am one of the few who does not agree with what has been done to the child and what they plan to do with her."

"Are you willing to betray your own people?" Darwin scoffed in disbelief.

"I am trying to help them from making a mistake they will later regret."

"I was unaware your kind had any relationship with the Newids."

Imogen glanced at Gundrel. "There was to be a celebration held for the pregnancy and the Newids were invited because-"

"They do not need to know the reason," Gundrel interrupted roughly.

They remained awkwardly silent until, finally, after thirty minutes of walking, Imogen said, "We're here."

Through the trees ahead, Gavin and Darwin could make out a house. It was a gorgeous place, with white-washed walls, bay windows, and a slate roof. It rose two stories high and climbing roses crept up the walls, looking slightly underkept. The wooden front doors were nestled between two wooden trellises and were slightly ajar. The group made their way past the cobbled pathway leading to the house and peered through the doors. All was still except for the flickering of four short candles on a wooden table in the hall. The Enchantress entered first, followed close behind by Gundrel, then Darwin and Gavin, who jostled the former to get through first.

They stood in a narrow hallway of white wooden floors and grey-blue painted walls; everything from the floors to the walls to the stairway leading up to the right spoke of comfort and simplicity. But, Darwin had to admit, it felt cold, unwelcoming, as though the house knew he was not meant to be there.

Imogen led them swiftly through the house. She made her way down the hall and turned into a room at the end of the hallway with Gundrel, Darwin, and Gavin following quickly behind. They entered a small, dimly lit room with a red-carpeted floor and cream-coloured walls. Heavy drapes curtained the windows, shielding the room from view from the outside. In the middle, far end of the room, behind a simple set of furniture sat a large four-poster double bed and in front of the bed, leaning heavily against the one post, stood an Enchantress who was almost identical to Imogen, with the same dark hair and purple eyes, but she was slightly shorter and curvier. She wore a long white nightgown that stretched against her enlarged belly, which she clutched, groaning. She glanced up as they entered and relief flooded her pinched, sweaty face. She looked ready to faint, so Imogen ran up to her and held her arm.

"Are you okay, Rebecca?" Imogen's face was lined with worry as she helped her mistress to sit on the bed. "Why were you standing?"

"The baby," she whispered, as though utterly drained, "She's coming." She moaned, biting down on her hand to keep from screaming.

Imogen nodded. "Lie down and take deep breaths. Would you like me to ease the pain?"

"No, no, the baby, there's no time." She groaned again, letting out a long breath. She looked at Imogen with utter fear and panic. "I don't know if I can do this."

"You can. I'm here with you." Imogen pushed Rebecca back onto the bed, propping her head with a pillow.

"He should be here, too: the father." Tears started streaking down her face and she began panting as another contraction wracked her body.

Imogen nodded. "I know, but Gundrel is here in his place." She looked around and beckoned Gundrel, who moved to Rebecca's side and held her hand, grimacing as she clutched it back tightly. Then Imogen said to the two men, "I need you two to fetch blankets and towels from the closet in the bathroom outside." They looked at her for a few seconds then both nodded and went to get their respective things, seemingly relieved to be leaving the room.

Imogen turned back to Rebecca and said, "Bend your legs up - I need to see the baby." Rebecca shut her eyes and moaned, but did as she was told. Imogen nodded. "I can see her head. I want you to pull your legs up with your arms, and when you feel the next contraction, push. Ready?"

Rebecca nodded, fear lining her face. Then she groaned.

"Push!" said Imogen, gently, but forcefully. Rebecca screwed up her face and, pulling at her legs, pushed as hard as she could. She gritted her teeth to keep from screaming and sweat and tears trickled down her face. Three more times she pushed. After each push, she collapsed back, gasping and sobbing, absolutely drained.

"One more, Rebecca. You can do it."

The two men returned, Darwin holding towels, and Gavin's arms balancing an unnecessarily tall tower of blankets. They brought them forward toward the bed, stopping dead at the sight before them. Darwin's face drained of colour and Gavin looked ready to throw up. Imogen grabbed a towel and placed it at the bottom of the bed, ready to catch the child.

And then the baby was there. After one final push, Rebecca collapsed back, panting, pale and pasty.

"Well done, Rebecca," said Gundrel, as he looked over to see the child. Her eyes, the same shade as her mother's, were open and she stared at Imogen as she was picked up and passed to the mother. Rebecca smiled slightly and brushed her hands over the girl's mop of dark hair.

Imogen grabbed a fluffy white blanket from Gavin and draped the blanket over the baby. Then she turned reluctantly to Rebecca, who was smiling down at the girl.

"Rebecca," she started.

"I know," interrupted Rebecca, sorrow in her voice. She then looked at the four of them and said with force that didn't match her tired expression, "She cannot remain here and the queen must never find out where she is, or we shall all be doomed." Tears started streaking down her face and she leaned down to kiss the girl. "All four of you are charged with her care. You will take her far away from here and care for her as though she were your own. She cannot know who she is, how important she is, not until she is ready."

They all nodded. Imogen took the child carefully into her arms. Rebecca stared at the baby, tears now streaming down her face. She quickly pulled something from her bedside table and passed it to

Imogen: a small black box. Imogen took it and the Enchantress, Newid, and two men, turned to leave, ready to start their long trek as far from this place of darkness and evil as possible.

Just as they reached the door, Rebecca called out. "Wait!" she cried. "Her name!" They turned to look at Rebecca one last time. "Her name is Elowen. Elowen Farrowspire."

Chapter 2

Elowen Farrowspire

Thousands of miles from the village of Milas, over the vast, icy tips of Feinberg mountain, across the misty, muddy marsh of Fellmoor and through the rocky desert of the Inah Waste, lay the sprawling city of Illfang of Lord Kobold. Its fortified walls were nestled between the two rivers of Tydh and Mistfen, and the tall, black, stone keep and castle of Braburh, perched upon the city's topmost hill, overlooked the glittering Sea of Apias and was surrounded by beautiful, white mansions of the Upper Section. While Illfang's strategic position had a wild beauty about it, the city itself, with its distinct separation between the rich and the poor, was not so idyllic. It was a city where the rich families squabbled over their political positions while the poor fought for a place among the many gangs that ran rampant in the city. With opportunities scarce and food even more so, there was an atmosphere of greed and desperation that permeated deeper than the sewerage that spilt across the streets of the poverty-stricken Lower Section.

Deep within the dirt and squalor of the Lower Section, in a part that felt out of place in such a dangerous city, was a safe haven for the abandoned children who had swarmed the streets: a home painted in vibrant colours of red, yellow and blue, and filled with laughter. It was a fairly new addition to the city, formed only nineteen years ago by a beautiful woman of unknown origins. She went by the name of Mistress Monige and though she had so selflessly established the only home for children ridden by poverty, people still avoided her, for her strange dark purple-black hair and purple eyes made most of the men and women of the city uncomfortable. No race had passed through the city with such distinctive features as hers, or that of the young girl who was often seen with the mistress - one of the first foundlings in the home - who went by the name of Elowen.

She, too, was avoided by all but the children of the home, for she had the same abnormal purple eyes, and while a few people believed the rumour that Elowen was the illegitimate daughter of Mistress Monige, most scoffed at the idea; the only similarities between the two women were their eyes and pale skin. While the Mistress was tall, and, according to most men in the city, absolutely gorgeous, the girl was slight in an underfed kind of way, with a slim face and long, pale, shimmering silver hair that was often tied with a black ribbon into a ponytail. She might have been called pretty had she not made most people feel uneasy with her silence and seriousness. She barely spoke and rarely smiled, unless she was with the other foundlings. She was too strange to be called beautiful and too different to be welcomed into any circle.

Her appearance wasn't the only thing keeping the rest of the Lowers at bay. Rumours about the girl, and the Mistress, had begun to spread slowly but surely through the Lower Section when, from an early age, she had been seen practising archery at the back of the Foundlings' Home. This caused quite a stir among the mothers living in the surrounding houses who could not fathom why a child the same age as their little ones would be doing such an unladylike and dangerous activity.

"Quite irresponsible!" They could often be heard saying to each other as they stood outside their houses, watching their children running about, though never too close to 'that Foundling Girl'. On the rare occasions that Elowen had left her archery practice to wander the streets of the Lower Section, the other children had been warned not to associate with Elowen, lest they get any funny ideas.

Soon, however, the Lowers had lost interest in the mistress and her first foundling as the years passed and they became ordinary, old news. Though she still practised archery regularly, she began taking up other, 'irresponsible' hobbies. She would often be seen throwing knives at targets, followed by weapon practice, usually a rapier, as well as a strange activity that was realised was combat training.

While her skills became unrivalled in the Lower Section, she was soon viewed not with disgust or discomfort, but rather fear and anger. Some of the residents of the Lower Section began plotting to rid the city of what they saw as a threat to their very existence: Elowen.

"Stupid, paranoid, that's all they are," the Mistress had told Elowen once word reached them. And while Elowen had been warned not to leave the Foundling Home unnecessarily, the stubborn and easily bored girl continued to roam the streets. Then, one night, on her fourteenth birthday, Elowen had been outside the Foundling Home, wandering the streets of the labyrinth of the Lower Section, when she was attacked by four men. It was an exciting story, one told around the fire at the local tavern the very next day.

"She gutted them in one move," cried one patron of the Tavern.

"Idiot!" cried another. "They're not dead - I saw them this very morning."

There had been much shouting and arguing and while nobody could quite agree on the story at first, it was eventually decided that the girl could not have been alone, but how she'd done it remained a mystery. Only one old man with deeply wrinkled skin and narrow, beady eyes, seemed to have witnessed the event yet told a most ludicrous and unbelievable story.

"She changed! There was a bright light and she changed! I saw her with my own eyes! She was a great beast!"

Again and again, he said this, to much howling laughter, but when the patrons of the tavern wanted to get the man back to tell his wickedly funny and ridiculous story, the man could not be found.

Whatever the story was, and it was most frustrating that the men who had attacked Elowen had no recollection of the event whatsoever, one thing was certain: the girl was not to be meddled with.

And so she was still avoided, but Elowen stopped being the talk of the town after some time. That is until she turned sixteen and moved out of the Foundlings' Home. As an ember fanned into flames, rumours spread across the city as though its inhabitants had nothing better to do than talk about Elowen. Especially when her daily activities changed.

Indeed, it became her daily routine to go hunting, which left most people baffled. Food was expensive nowadays, as it was well-known and often talked about in the Lower Section, but never before had they seen anyone hunt for food, particularly when the Foundlings' Home was one of the more well-to-do residences in the Lower Section and her new lodging, the Dastardly Boar, was even less affected by the sudden food price hikes. Nevertheless, once Elowen had relocated to the housing above the most popular tavern in the Lower Section, the residents around the Foundlings' Home could expect to see Elowen early each morning leaving the squalor of the city, a longbow and quiver of arrows strapped across her back, for a trip into the woods surrounding the city. It was not uncommon to see her returning with rabbits or fowls that, it was said, would be given to the poorer families who couldn't afford food. Very strange behaviour, according to most families, and even the homeless. They decided she was still not to be trusted or befriended.

But then there was something else that made it even more imperative that she be avoided, something the citizens of the Lower Section knew, and Elowen did not: that she was protected by the Shikari.

An ancient Guild charged with the protection of the Kingdom of Arantaea from the evil magical creatures that had appeared shortly after the War of Eternal Regret centuries before, the Shikari's main stronghold resided only a few kilometres East of Illfang in Palmor Tower. Of the six leaders, Lord Matterson could occasionally be seen in the Lower Section, watching the young girl from a distance and even once or twice conferring with the Mistress.

Why the Shikari had taken such an interest in the girl or why they had sent one of their most feared and despised leaders to keep watch over her was anybody's guess. But one thing was for sure: if the monster-hunter's guild was watching her, it was best that she be avoided. This belief was firmly established after Elowen, who was seventeen at the time, received her first invitation from the Shikari to enter the Marasae Tournament, a tournament usually held for those of the Upper Section.

Had she known, the people wondered, that she would be chosen to participate in the Tournament that would decide if she was fit to join the Shikari? And suddenly, a rumour started that Elowen would be the one to bring down the Uppers, perhaps even Lord Kobold himself. Hope began to spread like never before, hope that the Lowers had a chance of being something more.

"Soon," they would often say, "soon, the Uppers will realise they can't ignore us forever.

And so, in the years that had passed since Mistress Monige's arrival, Elowen was still shunned by most of the people of the Lower Section, though now she was revered rather than just feared. Even so, this day, the day of the Choosing, was going to prove that, even in the Upper Section, she was unwelcome, and the one question that had plagued the Lowers for twenty years would soon reach the Uppers: who is Elowen Farrowspire?

Chapter 3

An Invitation

In the middle of the Lower Section, a tavern could be found, the wooden sign outside it rocking in the wind reading, 'The Dastardly Boar'. Through the window of the tiny lodging above this popular tavern, the early morning sunshine streamed, dust particles danced in the warm beam of light, and an orange glow was cast on the opposite wooden floor and wall. The faded, tattered yellow-flowered curtains fluttered in the slight breeze, wafting in the smell of sewerage and smoke. Through the window, the many sounds indicative of that neighbourhood could be heard: the drunken laughter from the alehouse, the shout of a young man begging for food, and the seductive calls of women from the local brothel across the street.

A woman of twenty years sat on one of the three pieces of furniture in the room: a wooden stool at a small wooden desk placed between the rickety, brown-linen bed and the wooden door beside which leaned a longbow and quiver with three arrows. The desk looked out of the window onto the dirty, narrow street outside and though she was close enough to the buildings across the road to see into them, they were slightly blocked from view by the linen and clothing hanging on the lines strung across the street. Her head rested lazily on the palm of her left hand and she drummed the table with the fingers of her other hand as she stared absentmindedly at the paper in front of her. It was a letter, printed on expensive parchment in big bold letters and read:

EXCLUSIVE INVITE

His High Lord Kobold and
Master Gimrad Drovenshere
invite you to partake in the annual
Marasae Tournament
on the Eve of the Autumn Solstice
at The Labyrinth of Marasae.

The rest of the letter was covered by an expensive red envelope with the name 'Elowen Farrowspire' etched in gold on the front.

Elowen stood up and stretched, her too-small, faded green, secondhand dress lifting high above her muddied boots, and her short, brown coat pulling taught against the buttons stitched down her front. She had the appearance of a woman unable to come to terms with her coming of age and unwilling, or unable, to buy new clothes to better fit her change in body. The only thing that appeared to be new was a dainty silver locket that hung on a chain around her neck, disappearing into her slight cleavage.

A knock on the door made Elowen start. She looked around just as the door opened and in stepped a girl who looked to be a little older than Elowen. She had slightly greasy, black hair, slanted, grey eyes, and thin lips, and had a more muscular appearance to Elowen, though her pale blue dress accentuated her slight curviness. She had a sweet face and she beamed when she saw Elowen. This girl's name was Hally Marsin and she was the best and only friend of Elowen Farrowspire.

Hally quickly shut the door behind her and leaned back against it, saying breathlessly, "You received it again, didn't you?" She had a high voice with a heavy accent that accentuated the 'r' and shortened the vowels.

Elowen smiled and replied in a soft voice with a similar, but less heavy, accent, "Yes, it came this morning. Same delivery man, too. He had the gall to look irritated that he was delivering the letter to me for the fourth year in a row. And, you won't believe what he said."

Hally's grin deepened and her eyes sparkled, "Let me guess: 'Please just do the damn tournament!'"

Elowen laughed, "You were listening, weren't you?" This did not surprise Elowen in the least. Hally's only fault was that she was incredibly inquisitive, or, as most people liked to call her, annoyingly nosy. That, coupled with the fact that she worked at the tavern, meant that she knew everything about everybody.

Hally shrugged, then lifted her eyebrow questioningly, "Well, are you going to do it this time?"

Sinking onto the bed, Elowen bit her lip in thoughtfulness. "Maybe," she eventually replied. "I still don't know why they asked me; I'm from the Lower Section."

"Plus you're a girl-"

"There are many girls in the Tournament," Elowen interrupted, raising her eyebrows.

"Let me finish." Hally held up her hand. "You're a girl who could never compete against the likes of the other girls in the Tournament, which is probably good because they all look like they could crush you with a friendly hug."

"Thanks," Elowen replied sarcastically, then grinned. "I might not be as strong, but I'm sure that I'm faster."

Hally giggled. "And smarter. Oh, go for it, El! Last year you made excuses, even though you then trained like crazy. Don't give me that look. You know I know everything that you do. I mean, we practically live in each other's faces. So what's the harm in trying, El?"

"Dying, perhaps?"

"That was one time, and that guy was an idiot."

"Hal!"

Hally blushed as though suddenly realising what she'd said. "Sorry, you know what I mean. Anyway, what I'm trying to say is that you have as good a chance as any to get into the Shikari. No one will pay any attention to you; they'll see you as the scrawny, sickly one who poses no threat to them."

Elowen laughed. "Thanks, Hal." She leaned her head back against the wall, bits of splintered wood catching on her hair. "There's still a possibility it's just a joke or an accident."

Hally rolled her eyes, "Four years of invitations for a joke or a mistake? Come on, El. You can't still think that. As shocking and scary as it might be, it's time you considered the possibility it's not a mistake."

"Yeah, I guess you're right," Elowen replied, sighing. "It's quite a conundrum."

"No, it's not, though I will admit it is curious. I, for one, would like to know why they chose you and the only way we'll figure that out is if you go and 'do the damn tournament.'" She grinned and winked.

Elowen laughed. "Okay, okay. But I still don't have a partner. Nobody from the Lower Section is going to want to help me and I know no one from the Upper Section... nor do I trust any of them."

"How about this," started Hally, pushing away from the door and squeezing next to Elowen on the small bed. "I will allow you to enter me as the person carrying your gear - your partner."

Elowen's eyes widened in surprise and she pushed forward off the wall and stared at Hally. "You'd do that?" she asked. "Why? What if we die?"

"Again, that happened once." She held up her hand, stopping Elowen from interrupting. Lifting her chin, she said, "It's my decision. And you've said it yourself: It's time we stop being sidelined. I'm tired of being ignored just because I'm not an Upper, and I know you are, too. Otherwise, why would you have been practising so hard these last few years? It's time to stop procrastinating, take that training, and go show the Uppers we're worthy of being included."

Elowen nodded, then threw her arms around Hally. "Thank you," she whispered. Then she pulled back, frowning. "But what about your work? Bartholomew might not be so keen on his best barmaid being gone for so many days."

Hally shrugged. "He owes me for helping him find his ale-thief." She paused suddenly, smacking her forehead with her hand. "Oh, and I almost forgot, Mistress Monige is looking for you."

"Why?" asked Elowen warily. She tried to recall if she had done something wrong; Mistress Monige rarely asked to see Elowen now that she had moved out of the orphanage.

Hally shrugged and replied, "It sounded like a friendly invitation, but I would still get going if I were you." Without another word, Hally stood and skipped out the door, not bothering to close it.

Elowen sighed and focused on her stomach which was still churning with nerves, but a new resolve pulled her to her feet. Grabbing the letter and stuffing it back in its envelope, she stalked out the door with her newfound confidence into the tiny hall outside, and down the dark and narrow staircase leading to the bar.

It was busy so early in the morning, with both hungover patrons from the night before, and new customers seeking to drink their troubles away. The hum of talk filled the room, with the occasional booming laugh echoing across the tavern. The place itself was a large, low-roofed wooden room with few windows and even fewer candles, both fighting to chase the shadows away. Twenty or so tables had been squeezed into the room with five stools packed around each, and most were occupied by groups of men. In the front of the alehouse was the wooden bar that had many empty wooden ale mugs, a dirty cloth, and several dusty bottles of ale atop it. Behind the bar stood a man: Bartholomew Gorning.

Bartholomew, the owner of the tavern, was a beefy man with beady eyes and a massive beard and moustache. He had laugh lines all across his weathered face and he stood behind the bar with his arms crossed across his apron, listening to Hally as she told him her plans with much enthusiastic gesturing. His mouth twitched and he pursed his lips as though struggling to keep a straight face. Eventually, he nodded, causing Hally to let out a great 'whoop' and hug Bartholomew around the middle (he was such a big man that her head hardly reached his chin and her arms barely fit around his middle).

Hally turned and saw Elowen, and she held her thumbs up. Bartholomew raised his eyebrows at Elowen as Hally nearly ran the short distance to her, slipping slightly on the dusty stone floor, and grabbing Elowen's arm to steady herself. Elowen giggled.

"Are you sure your clumsiness will handle such a treacherous place as the Labyrinth?" asked Elowen, grinning.

"Oh har har," Hally replied and rolled her eyes. Then, she eyed Elowen seriously, grabbing her by both shoulders and pulling her close. "You need to do this, El. We need someone who will give us some kind of hope."

Elowen nodded. "The Uppers cannot ignore us forever." It sounded like a mantra, like something she had repeated over and over.

Hally smiled encouragingly and pushed Elowen back, a little roughly, and said, "Go. And don't come back unless you've signed up."

Outside the inn, the sudden brightness stunned Elowen. She blinked rapidly as her eyes grew accustomed to the light. There was an icy briskness in the air and Elowen shivered slightly. She was used to the many smells of the Lower Section, but she still wrinkled her nose as a strong breeze pulled at her hair and dress. She stepped down off the front step and her boots immediately squelched in the mixture of mud and excrement. Beggars looked in her direction, but she turned away from them and began making her way through the narrow, winding streets of the Lower Section toward the orphanage.

The short route she took soon brought her to the front of the Home for Foundlings as the sun slowly crept towards its apex. The tall and colourful building loomed in front of her and she smiled as she saw children running in the small, dusty area before the orphanage. Memories flashed through her mind, both of happy and hard times,

Though she knew she had grown up blessed to be cared for by the mistress, the pressure put on her shoulders to train had always made the happy times seem short-lived.

The children waved as they saw Elowen then promptly continued with their game of tag. Elowen walked to the front door, which was open and swinging in the slight breeze that brought with it the smell of the sea. She took a deep, comforting breath and made her way inside, blinking as her eyes grew accustomed to the dark hall. Up the stairs, to the left of the hall, she went, past several windows looking out onto the yard outside, and to the office of Mistress Monige.

The room she entered was dimly lit. The mistress had spared no expense with the furnishings: the walls had been painted a pretty blue, the colour of the sea on a gloomy day, and a fire was blazing in a small fireplace to her right, surrounded by comfortable deep-green couches. To her left, the wall was lined with bookcases, and toward the end of the room was a long, wooden desk with an orb of light hovering over it. Behind the desk were two chairs, Mistress Monige seated in one, the other occupied by another young and slightly plump woman who went by the name of Mistress Fenagry. Mistress Monige wore a long black dress and looked exactly the same as she always did: intimidating, but absolutely gorgeous and not a day older than when she had arrived in the Lower Section. Fenagry wore a soft purple dress, tight around her large belly. Mistress Monige and Mistress Fenagry looked up as Elowen entered and shut the door, Mistress Monige's stern face relaxing into a tight smile while the other mistress gave Elowen a small wave.

"Ah, Elowen," said Mistress Monige. "Good. You got my message." She turned to look at Mistress Fenagry and said, "Thank you, dear. You may go now. And make sure Mistress Sunning has given the children their lunch, will you?"

Mistress Fenagry nodded and quickly stood from her seat.

"Do you want me to put these in the storage room?" she asked, holding up the pieces of parchment she was holding.

"No, leave them here. I'll do it."

Mistress Fenagry left the room, patting Elowen on the shoulder as she passed. Elowen sat down in the cushioned pale pink chair in front of the desk as the door to the office closed with a soft click. She waited as the Mistress finished writing something on the parchment in front of her, Elowen slowly drumming her fingers on the wooden sides of the chair. Eventually, Mistress Monige looked up, rolling up the parchment slowly.

"How are you feeling, my girl?"

Elowen shrugged. "Alright, I guess. I got the letter again."

"I know."

Elowen smiled. "You know everything that goes on in this place, don't you, Mistress?"

"I try to make a point of knowing what happens to my favourite girl. Now, have you decided yet?"

Elowen bit her cheek, looking at her hands. She had been sure when she had been at the tavern with Hally, but now that she was alone she couldn't help doubting her decision.

Mistress Monige sighed, as though she could see what Elowen was thinking. "It's time, El. We can no longer put it off. You are ready, child. I can no longer help you. You must enter the tournament."

Elowen frowned and said, "Well, I was planning to, but-"

"You need to enter this year, El."

"Why?" asked Elowen, frowning at Mistress Monige's tone of urgency.

The mistress stood up from her chair and moved to the bookcase. Reaching for a particularly large green book, she took it out, put her hand into the gap and Elowen heard something click. Part of the bookshelf opened like a door to a small space out of which the mistress took something. Making her way back to the desk, she sat down again and placed a black box on the desk in front of Elowen.

"Open it," she ordered softly.

Confused, Elowen reached toward the box, pausing before she touched it. She felt sure she could hear a soft, almost indistinguishable thumping, like the beat of a relaxed heart. The box was cold to the touch as Elowen's fingers brushed against it. Pulling at the lid, it slid off with a small sigh. Frowning, Elowen peered inside and gasped. She glanced up to find the mistress considering her carefully.

"It is called an Ornette," the mistress said softly and pushed the box toward Elowen, who stared at it in wonder and awe.

It was a necklace with a golden eye hanging from it, about the size of the palm of her hand. The iris was a red ruby, with two long pieces of gold intersecting in the shape of an 'x' behind the ruby and jutting out slightly from the top and bottom of the eye. It was an exquisite piece of jewellery that glittered in the light of the orb above the mistress. Elowen reached for the necklace, then jumped back with a yelp as it blinked at her.

"It moved!" she cried, looking up at the mistress in surprise.

The mistress nodded. "Yes, dear, but there's no need to be afraid. Put it on."

Elowen gingerly reached for it again and put it around her neck, removing the locket that had been hanging from her neck. It was a cold weight, but not uncomfortable. It pressed against her chest with a familiarity that Elowen couldn't place, yet she felt a sense of warmth spread through her from it, as though it welcomed her as a wearer. A shiver ran through Elowen.

"An Ornette," said the mistress, "Is very rare and should never be removed, and it should remain hidden beneath your clothes at all times."

"Where did you get it," asked Elowen, fingering it gently as though it were a living thing.

"From your mother."

Elowen glanced up quickly, dropping the Ornette so that it was hidden beneath her dress, "Excuse me?"

"It is your coming-of-age gift."

Elowen frowned, then said, "I came of age six years ago."

The mistress shook her head, "For humans, yes, but as a half-Enchantress, half-Newid, coming of age only happens when you turn twenty."

"A half-what?" whispered Elowen, her eyes wide with surprise.

"You heard me. It is time I tell you-"

The door to the study opened suddenly and two giggling girls entered. They stopped as they saw Elowen and blanched as they saw the Mistress's face. Both girls wore the same outfit as Elowen, though smaller to fit their tiny bodies, and their brown hair was tied back.

"M-m-miss," stuttered the one, nervously wringing her hands. "That man is here to see you: Lord Matterson."

The mistress's eyes widened and she stood up quickly, her chair pushed back so suddenly that it fell over backwards, hitting the carpet with a thud. She quickly shuffled some papers on her desk and then turned to Elowen, a harried expression on her face.

"We will talk later, Elowen," she said, frowning. "It is important that you know... everything. Now go sign up and good luck."

She hurried out the door, pulling the two girls after her and leaving Elowen slightly bewildered. She got up slowly and made her way back downstairs. She was tempted to see the man who had come to see the mistress, but she knew that if she was to sign up, she needed to get going.

Taking a deep breath, feeling the Ornette pulsing gently against her chest, she began her trek toward the Keep of Brahbur.

Chapter 4

The Shikari Lord

The Upper half of the city was separated from the Lower Section by a tall, stone wall, both in an attempt to keep out the ruffians as well as to hide the stain upon the land that was the Lower Section. It helped the rich pretend the poor did not exist and it gave the poor all the more reason to hate the rich. The only way into the richer section was a portcullis that separated the cobbled and clean main road of the Upper Section from the dirty and dusty main road of the Lower Section, which was hustling and bustling with activity: people carrying their wares, adults begging for coin and children playing with a dirty ball. Three guards stood at the gate, wearing a deep red and black guard outfit and armed with halberds. When Elowen finally arrived on the busy main road after an hour of winding her way through the many sideroads, she walked towards the entryway. The guards immediately barred the entrance with their halberds, causing her to pause, uncertainly.

Elowen eventually lifted her chin in steely determination, clutching the envelope tighter in her left hand, and the Ornette in her right, and stalked toward the guards.

"Halt," said the one guard. He was taller than the other two and had a balding head and thick, brown moustache, which bristled angrily as he stepped forward. He was obviously the superior of the three, having more coloured bars than the other two, younger guards. They both had dark skin and eyes, which were narrowed, and they remained where they were behind the older man.

Elowen stopped a few feet away, then took one cautious step forward and said loudly and clearly, "I ask for permission to pass to-"

"No persons may enter without the required paperwork and identity documents," interrupted the older man.

"I have an invitation from Lord Kobold-" started Elowen again.

The younger guard on the left snorted and he sneered as he looked the girl up and down. "I highly doubt that."

Elowen blushed, then held up the red envelope, and both younger guards exchanged a glance and then burst out laughing. The older guard smiled sardonically and said, "You expect us to believe the High Lord Kobold sent you an invitation?"

Elowen pursed her lips and narrowed her eyes in anger. "This letter was sent to me this morning, as it has been every morning for the past five years. If you would just look at it, you would see it is an invitation to enter the Marasae Tournament."

The older guard let out a bark of laughter. "The Tournament is for the people of the Upper Section only. Go home and stop wasting our time."

He was about to turn away when his eyes suddenly widened and his gaze focused on something behind Elowen.

"My Lord," he said quickly, fear suddenly coating his voice. He gave a quick bow. Confused, Elowen turned to look behind her and jumped slightly when she saw a man standing behind her; she hadn't heard him approach. He was a tall and skinny man, with a mop of sandy hair and small eyes that flashed in anger. He wore black breeches and a black tunic with a sheathed broadsword bucked to his belt. There was a silver badge of a sword piercing monstrous wings under his left shoulder, covered slightly by the heavy, long, black cloak he wore over his back. Her eyes widened as she recognized it; the symbol of the Shikari.

E lowen took a quick step back, then suddenly became acutely aware that she was now alone on the main road surrounded by four men; the activity that had filled the street had suddenly stopped, the people immediately disappearing into the shadows with the arrival of this new man.

"My Lord," said the older man again, "we were just trying to stop her from passing without the necessary pass papers."

"Let her through," the new man said softly, surprising Elowen.

"But my Lord-"

"Didn't you hear her? She has an invitation to the Tournament."

The older guard sneered slightly and replied, "My Lord, you cannot possibly believe her. She is from the Lower Section." His nose wrinkled in disgust.

"And yet I can see the invitation quite clearly." He looked at Elowen and held out his hand. She reluctantly handed over the invitation, clutching it tightly for a few seconds before letting go as he tugged at it.

The new man opened the letter and began to read, "A formal invitation to... let's see..." He turned the envelope over to look at the front. "To Elowen Farrowspire." The new man glanced at Elowen briefly, curiously, before turning his attention back to the letter. "This letter is clearly an invitation to the Marasae Tournament." When the guards still seemed hesitant and reluctant to let them through, the new man's expression darkened and he stepped past Elowen and, with a swiftness that surprised her, he suddenly stood before the guards. Even the guards took a step back in fear.

"If you will not let her pass with an official invitation," he began, so quietly that Elowen could barely hear him, "then you will let her pass with me as her escort."

The guards exchanged a glance and finally nodded. As they stepped to the side, the older guard bowed his head and said, grudgingly, "As you wish, my lord."

The new man looked back at Elowen. "I will escort you to the Black Keep of Brahburh," he said and gestured for her to follow him. Elowen hesitated as he set off at a brisk pace. As he passed under the wrought-iron gate, a sudden bustle of activity filled the main street behind Elowen, as though it had never stopped. Beggars again began calling for money and food, wagons continued carrying their wears and the hum of talk filled the road once more. Everyone eyed Elowen and kept a wary distance from her.

The man paused at the gate and, without turning, said loudly, "Follow me."

Elowen stared at him, trying to determine the worth of following him or making a run for it. It did not seem she had much of a choice; go home with the disappointing news that she had not signed up, or follow this unknown man who seemed keen to help her. When the man turned and looked at her questioningly, Elowen sighed and decided the latter option was the best.

She began walking quickly to catch up with the man. As she passed the glaring guards, Elowen gave in to temptation and smirked at them. The older guard's eyes flashed in anger and he said softly, "You smell as bad as you look, rat."

Elowen stopped and considered him. Her resolve to compete grew. She reminded herself of the power she would have, the influence, to have people respect her and stop seeing her as just another Lower. And so she said, "When I get into the Shikari, you will be the first monster I hunt." She turned without another word and stalked off toward the man, who, she noticed, wore a small smile. "What?" she asked, a little more sharply than she intended.

The man shrugged and said, "I'm just impressed by your confidence... or is it arrogance?"

"Who are you anyway?" she demanded as they began walking together through the main street.

"Call me Darwin."

"You are Shikari."

"Correct." He paused as he realised Elowen had stopped again. He looked back at her and found her staring in wonderment at the sights around her.

"You've never been here before," he stated, realisation mingled with surprise.

"Obviously, not," she replied, her eyes wide. "It's... beautiful."

Homes lined the main street, with steeply pitched gabled roofs, intricate masonry chimneys, ornate doorways and windows, and embellishing half-timbering spaced with white stucco. Flower boxes hung from the window sills containing dainty asters, colourful gladiolus and soft dahlias. They had left the smell of sewerage behind and were met with a freshness and cleanliness the likes of which had never been seen in the Lower Section.

People milled around, beautiful ladies walking in pairs, wearing soft, flowing frocks and holding dainty parasols. The men wore tan breeches, decorated, deep-coloured tunics and black boots. Both men and women frowned and glowered at Elowen, giving her a wide berth, while nodding politely at Darwin. Elowen was so focused in amazement at the sights around her that she barely noticed their rudeness.

She sighed and smiled sadly. "I had no idea this is what money can buy. It makes me wish I could snap my fingers and have the Lower Section be just as stunning."

Darwin tilted his head and said, "Don't be fooled. They lack in different ways and, too, require our pity."

Elowen rolled her eyes. "I'm sure having so much food and money must be a very hard life indeed."

Laughing, Darwin replied, "Oh, it cannot be likened to the Lower Section in the least, but don't think they don't have their own demons."

Pursing her lips, Elowen looked away. She did not agree, but she also did not see the worth in arguing with an Upper. Aside from that, she had just seen the path that lay ahead of them. The main road was split into several sections by steep stairways leading up to the Keep of Brahburh.

Elowen swore, causing Darwin to glance at her in surprise. "What," he asked, as they reached the first set of stairs and she stopped.

"Gosh, I feel exhausted just looking at these stairs." He smiled in amusement and she grimaced. "Alright, let's do this."

Elowen counted fifty stairs by the time they made it to the top of the first lot of stairs. She was already clutching at a stitch in her side. Darwin seemed to be holding back a laugh and instead said, "How do you expect to make it through the Tournament with endurance like that?"

She considered telling him that, had she not been practising, it would have been worse, but instead decided to keep her preparations a secret, hopefully to her benefit, "Well, to be honest, I only decided today to enter, so I haven't really prepared." The lie came easily because it was half true; she probably would have kept delaying her entry had it not been for Hally.

"What?!"

Elowen looked at Darwin in surprise as he grabbed her arm and pulled her to a sudden stop. The Ornette swung free of her dress and without thinking, she twisted her arm, freeing it, then punched him in the stomach. He doubled over slightly and coughed.

Frowning up at her, he said, "Well, at least you're not completely useless, then. I thought you would have at least done some training."

"I thought the invitation was a mistake." This, too, was mostly true; Lowers weren't included in the Tournament.

"Mistake? Five times? No endurance or brains, it seems," he grinned at her expression of outrage before continuing walking. Fuming, Elowen stalked after him.

"How do you know I was invited five times?" she said through gritted teeth.

He pointed at his chest where the badge of the Shikari glinted in the sun. "I thought that would be obvious. Well, that and the fact that I was one of the people to put you forward as a candidate."

Surprise flashed across Elowen's face and she stared at him, narrowly avoiding walking into a signpost at a cross-street. "You?"

"Me."

"Why? I thought only Uppers could participate."

"Not necessarily," he replied. "If you can give a good enough reason, you can nominate anybody."

"Why would you choose me? You don't even know me."

He coughed loudly. "Come on. We need to walk faster if we are to make it in time."

She opened her mouth, closed it, opened it again, and then said, "In time for the sign-up? I thought it would be all day."

"No, the sign-up is in the morning. The test is all day."

They had just reached the second lot of stairs and Elowen tripped slightly on the first one as her heart seemed to constrict. "A test?"

"Surely you read the invitation?" He frowned disapprovingly at her.

"Of course I did." They reached the last step and Elowen, breathing heavily, said, "I don't remember seeing that, though."

Darwin sighed. "It's a spoken exam-"

"Okay."

"- where they question your knowledge of magical creatures, and how to approach different magical situations. Did Mistress Monige cover that with you?"

"Well...." she replied, surprised by the mention of the mistress's name.

They had reached the final stairs and she began to notice the houses changing to beautiful white mansions adorned with decorative stone features and luscious gardens full of roses. But the beauty surrounding her could not mask the niggling feeling that she was missing something; something about what he had said did not fit.

She felt herself slowing as they reached the top and she stared at him. He seemed to know a lot more than would be expected of an Upper, let alone a Shikari. He also seemed to know a lot about her. Who was this man and what did he want from her? Before she could ask, a shadow passed over her and she looked up at the looming Keep of Brahburh.

They stood before a drawbridge that led over a moat to a gateway. It was another portcullis wedged in the middle of tall walls that surrounded the black Keep. Guardhouse towers rose on the corners and guards could be seen through the windows, on the battlement, and in the gatehouses. They made their way through, past more guards, who bowed to Darwin and frowned at Elowen, into the courtyard, a large, open area with many paths leading in different directions. There were short, long buildings on either side of the courtyard and at the far end stood the Keep. It towered above the cobbled area in front of it, a tall, rectangular building with towers at each corner. It was both impressive and intimidating. And behind it loomed the castle of Brahburh with its embellished stone walls and high turrets. Red and white flags flapped in the wind with the symbol of rearing horses.

There were many young people milling about in front of the Keep, talking in groups. The women and men all wore expensive-looking breeches and tunics of different colours and all looked big and strong enough to crush a bear. Elowen patted her dress down self-consciously and smoothed her hair. Her heart started hammering in her chest.

"Calm down," whispered Darwin sideways to her. "Try not to draw too much attention to yourself.

Elowen bit her lip and whispered back, "Too late."

Silence had fallen across the courtyard as everyone turned to look in their direction. Distaste, then surprise, flashed across their faces as they took in the two of them, looking from Elowen to Darwin. The sound of murmuring filled the area and Elowen nervously glanced around. She had never felt so different, or so unwelcome.

Darwin led the way past the people and, just before they reached the Keep, he turned right toward one of the shorter buildings, and the longest. It was built with a mixture of stones and wood and the large double wooden doors stood open leading into what appeared to be a mess hall. There were about twenty long tables with long benches on opposite sides. A large fireplace stood to the one side crackling merrily and heating the entire room and the fire, along with the candelabre, cast a warm glow on the walls. At the far end of the room was the longest table slightly raised above the others. Five bulky men, dressed in the same black tunic and breeches and sporting the symbol of the Shikari, sat on the wooden chairs behind it. They looked up as Darwin entered with Elowen trailing slightly behind him. She swallowed nervously as she took in the men seated at the front of the hall, then glanced at Darwin expectantly.

"Ah, Darwin," said the one in the middle with a gruff voice. "Do you finally have someone this year?"

"Yes," replied Darwin, smiling. "I present Elowen Farrowspire: my Champion for the Marasae Tournament."

Chapter 5

The First Test

The inner courtyard of the Keep of Brahburh grew steadily warmer as morning turned to afternoon. The sun beat down its blistering rays, while the cool wind provided brief respites from the heat. Elowen stood to one corner, barely listening to Darwin prattling away about the test. The shock she had felt when he had named her his champion still weighed heavily upon her shoulders, and she would not easily forget the look of outrage worn by most of the Shikari leaders after Darwin's announcement, a look shared by many of the other entrants waiting in the courtyard.

"Ignore them."

Darwin placed a hand on Elowen's shoulder, gently turning her towards him. Elowen bit her lip. She could still feel their stares burning into her back.

"This was a bad idea," she whispered, more to herself than Darwin.

Darwin shook his head. "You received the invitation just as they did; you have as much right to be here as they do."

Elowen struggled not to roll her eyes. "If only it were that simple. Even the leaders aren't happy."

"Not all of them are opposed to the idea." When Elowen didn't look convinced, Darwin continued, "You met only five of our six leaders today." He pulled her after him as he moved closer to one of the windows of the hall so they had a better view inside. Elowen couldn't help noticing how the other entrants immediately moved away from her. Through the window, the scene was much the same except for one of the entrants, a young boy with brown hair, standing in front of the long table in the front. Darwin began pointing out the different leaders.

"The man on the far side with olive skin and a scar across his face is Aavos. He is the weapons master and trainer and hails from the coastal city of Lidun. He is not opposed to a Lower entering, but he has never agreed with the decision to allow women to enter. A common problem with the Liduneans, unfortunately.

"The man beside him with golden skin and short, dark hair, stroking his goatee, is the head of accounts and coin. His name is Hahluk and he is from Enwick. As you should know, they are a people who deal in slavery and he has been petitioning for years to have the Lowers made slaves. Next to him, the man with the long face and even longer black hair, is Buze, head of the academy at Pamor Tower."

Darwin paused and pursed his lips as he glared at Buze. Elowen was surprised Buze could not feel the deadliness of that stare. Eventually, Darwin shook his head and continued, "The old man with shiny white hair is Wurtin, head historian and librarian. You will find no sympathy from him as he was there the last time a Lower was entered and will also remember what a disaster it was. Finally, the last man is Gavin, head of fieldwork and missions. He is not opposed to you being in the Tournament."

"And the sixth leader?" asked Elowen curiously.

"What about him?"

"Well, where is he?"

"As head of the Shikari, Gimrad is rarely seen," replied Darwin. "He's too busy to attend trivial events such as this."

"And is he against me entering the Tournament?"

Darwin looked at her, then, considering her intently. Eventually, he replied, "I cannot say for sure."

Elowen felt he was not being completely honest with her, but she nodded, then said, "Why is Gavin not opposed to me entering?"

"Oh, we're good friends. We used to be partners when we were sent on missions."

Elowen shook her head. "That doesn't answer my question." When Darwin looked away and didn't reply, she continued, "Why did you enter me as your champion, Darwin? You heard what Buze said."

"Which part?"

"That I am an unfit candidate, unlikely to be able to hold a sword, let alone wield one. I have no money even if I somehow complete the tournament without dying. Why me, a woman you don't even know?"

Darwin raised his eyebrow at her. "Surely Mistress Monige has told you why." When Elowen continued to look confused, he sighed, looking irritated, but before he could say anything, the door to the hall opened and a voice called out, "Elton Farron."

The boy who had been in the hall came out, worry lining his face and when he saw his sponsor, he shook his head dolefully and he and his sponsor made their way out of the Keep. The new boy, Elton, came forward and entered the hall, the door snapping shut with finality.

"You should be next," said Darwin quietly, looking after the boy who had just left the Keep.

"He didn't make it, did he?" asked Elowen quietly.

"And neither will you, rat," said a deep voice behind them.

Darwin and Elowen started and turned around. A young man, who looked to be the same age as Elowen, stood before them with his arms crossed. Behind him stood three other boys, though none of them were as bulky and strong as the first boy. They were all well-dressed in expensive-looking clothes and wore smirks across their faces as they looked Elowen up and down. The young man in the front had very short, light hair, a slight tan, and pale eyes, and Elowen might have thought him handsome had he not been wearing such an ugly look on his face.

Darwin stepped past Elowen and said, "What do you want?"

The young man glanced at Darwin and his smirk grew. "Ah, if it isn't Darwin of the Coven of the Dark Debacle." He turned back to Elowen. "You are lucky to be in the presence of such a failure of a Shikari. Oh, you didn't know?" He smiled at the look of consternation on Elowen's face. "You two make a great pair: the master who failed to kill the Coven of the Darks and the champion who will fail the Tournament." He spat on the ground. "Don't you think there are enough problems with the Lowers without making them think they are equal to us Uppers?" he snarled at Darwin. His face changed to one of hate and disgust as he stared at them both. Then he turned and left without another word, leaving both Elowen and Darwin in a state of shock.

"Well, that was unexpected." Darwin frowned after the young man.

"Who was that?" whispered Elowen, heat rushing to her cheeks.

"Rayan. He is a Shikari already, but he loves to come to the first test to scare the entrants."

"Shouldn't he show you some respect?"

Darwin smiled sardonically at Elowen. "You heard what he said; I'm seen as a failure in the eyes of the other Shikari. They believe it was my fault the war between the Enchantresses and the Newids and humans started."

"Was it?"

Darwin considered her carefully and eventually replied, rather forcefully, "No."

They fell into an awkward silence, eyeing the other entrants warily as though expecting them to approach, too. After some time, the doors opened again, the boy called Elton leaving with a smug grin on his face, and then Elowen's name echoed in the courtyard as she was called forth. Her hands trembled slightly and her legs didn't seem to want to move. Darwin eventually gave her a small push and said, "You'll be fine." The unsure undertone in his voice was not comforting, but Elowen made her way forward toward the doorway. A man in a guard's uniform stood to one side of the door, holding it open for her. He narrowed his eyes on her as she approached. She could almost feel the other champions glaring at her and following her every step. Elowen wiped her sweaty hands nervously down the sides of her dress and, as she passed through the doorway, she blinked rapidly till her eyes adjusted to the sudden lack of light. The door slammed shut behind her, making her jump slightly. She glanced toward the Shikari leaders and began to walk towards them, past the other tables and the fireplace, which now seemed to crackle ominously. Coming to a stop before them, she waited with bated breath, the Ornette pulsing steadily against her chest. She noticed they all wore the same outfit as Darwin with a shiny Shikari pin attached to their chests. They stared down at her with disapproving scowls, although she noted the man Darwin had called Gavin was looking at her with curiosity rather than animosity.

Buze spoke then. "You will be asked a series of questions by the leaders to determine your knowledge of survival, magical creatures, and other necessary information to become a Shikari. Should you pass this test," he smirked as though sure that she wouldn't, "you will be allowed to train for the tournament held in a fortnight."

She nodded, trying to appear more confident than she felt. She glanced towards the windows and saw Darwin peering through one of them. He nodded at her, and then he was gone. She noticed a few other champions gazing in at her. Feeling self-conscious, she turned back to the leaders.

Buze looked at Gavin and asked, "Shall we begin?" He pulled a quill and parchment toward him and began writing something down.

Gavin nodded, folding his hands in front of him and leaning forward slightly. "Right, Miss Farrowspire, first question: How would you identify and deal with a Jinx?"

Elowen breathed a sigh of relief. This was an easy question. She thought back to her conversations with Miss Monige and replied,

"They appear as wolves with fine, spiked, black hair and three, white eyes, and when they talk to you, you reply with questions."

She waited for Gavin to nod or shake his head, or give some sign as to whether her answer was correct or not, but he just moved on to the next question.

"Name and describe the main characteristics of five creatures you would need to avoid in the Necromancer's Waste."

She knew this answer, too. "The shadow creatures: the Millian and the Brillonder; the Necromancers' winged cat-familiars, Cirripir; the Waste Skeletons; and the insect-like creatures, Broxives."

Again, he gave no sign that she had answered correctly, causing Elowen to swallow nervously. He moved straight to the next question.

And so it went, each question much the same; focused on magical creatures, with a few general survival questions mixed in between. Finally, he asked one last question: "What is the best way to talk to the tree-like creature, a Hangu?", to which she answered: "Through riddles.", and Gavin leant back in his seat and looked to the historian, Wurtin. Wurtin immediately launched into his first question, speaking with a soft, wavering voice that Elowen could barely hear.

"Name the seven Enchantress families and how you would need to approach them should you require their help."

She nodded and began, counting on her fingers, "The Solar Enchantresses, the Coven of the Divine, the Wives of Ember, the Circle of Fortune, the Coven of the Twilight Grove, the Earthen Circle, and the Coven of the Dark Enchantresses. The first six should be offered services. The last coven should be avoided as any service given might end in death."

Wurtin's questions were more difficult, requiring Elowen to remember facts and dates of wars, names of important political factions and how to deal diplomatically with them, as well as main groups of peoples and races across Arantaea. She was mostly confident in her answers and replied to Wurtin's questions without too many pauses, but he, too, gave no sign as to whether she was correct or not. This began to frustrate Elowen, but she continued to answer, ending with Wurtin's last question: "The Desolation of Eshbash was caused by which recent war?" to which she replied, "The War of Fiendish Malice between the Enchantresses, Newids and humans."

Buze continued to make notes on his parchment but did not ask her any questions. Instead, Hahluk of accounts and coins began asking her about monetary values and accounts between the different races. These were, so far, the only questions she was not certain of her answers and a tightness began to squeeze at her chest as anxiety set in. She tried to remember as best she could the different currencies and conversions of neighbouring empires and kingdoms, the easiest to remember being her Arantaean currency of ten silver pieces to one gold piece, or one hundred copper pieces to one gold piece. She felt some relief when he asked his last question of which currency was the strongest and why, to which she replied, "The Newidian Empire, Raethenia, due to the mining of their mineral-rich mountainous land."

She felt some relief when they finally moved to Aavos for his questions on weapons and fighting styles. Elowen became very sure that she was answering all of his questions incorrectly, having never had the opportunity to fight or use weapons in real combat. Part of her had started not to care as she realised that she was almost done with her test.

Her heart leapt when he finally said, "Last question: what weapon would you choose for close combat?"

Answering with the first weapon that came to mind, she replied, "A rapier." She hoped she was correct. As with all the other leaders, he gave no indication whether her answer was right or not, instead letting silence fall as all the leaders turned to look at Buze, awaiting his judgment.

Buze considered her for a while, pursing his lips and stroking his thick beard. Elowen, beginning to feel uncomfortable with the silence, opened her mouth to ask whether she could leave, but, noticing Gavin give a small shake of his head made her close her mouth.

Eventually, after what felt like an age, Buze said, "You may go."

Elowen suppressed a nervous laugh, but could not stop herself from asking, "That's it?" After waiting so long for his verdict she felt a little let down by the shortness of his response. "Did I pass?"

Buze gave her a nasty smile. "Obviously not, or I would have given you details about the Tournament."

Elowen blushed. How was she to know that, she thought angrily, but said nothing. She was surprised by how disappointed she felt. Not wanting to spend another embarrassing minute in front of the leaders, she nodded, said a quiet 'thank you' and turned to leave. Out of the corner of her eye, she noticed Gavin leaning across Wurtin to whisper something to Buze. She hurried to the door and, as it opened, heard the name of the next champion called.

She found Darwin waiting for her outside and, finding the other champions watching her closely, she continued straight past Darwin at a brisk pace and gave no sign that she had failed. She couldn't stand the idea of the other champions knowing she had not passed the test. It was going to be bad enough facing Hally with this news, let alone having many of the Uppers know.

Darwin seemed to understand because he didn't say anything until they were outside the gate of the Keep.

"Did you -"

"Fail? Yes. Yes, I failed." Hot tears formed as anger and shame threatened to overwhelm her. She couldn't believe that after years of preparation and finally gathering the guts to enter, she hadn't even made it past the first round. Yet, she had been so sure she had gotten most of the questions correct. She found herself going over the questions again. Yes, she had felt certain about most of her answers and those she hadn't had been few and far between.

She sighed in frustration. "I knew this was a bad idea."

Darwin didn't say anything for a while. They began walking down the stairs leading from the Keep. Finally, he said, "I'll take you to the main gate and then say my goodbyes."

Elowen glanced at Darwin, surprised and a little hurt. "That's it?"

He shrugged. "That's it."

Fuming, she picked up her pace so that she was taking steps two at a time. "Well, don't let me keep you from your important work, Darwin. I can find my own way home."

He barked out a laugh, causing Elowen to almost trip down the last two stairs. She steadied herself then turned to glare at him.

"What's so funny?"

"You seem to be under the impression I am important enough to have work to do. Or that I'd rather do that than make sure you get back safely. Look." He held up her hand to stop her from interrupting him. "I'm not saying I'm not disappointed, but I do not blame you. I blame Imogen."

"Who?"

He just shook his head and started down the next lot of stairs. They continued in silence, Elowen's mind still on who Imogen might be until they reached the main gate. It seemed there had been a shift change as the guards who had been there were gone, replaced by two new guards with dark hair and skin. They nodded at Darwin and frowned at Elowen as they passed. When Darwin and Elowen reached the beginning of the Lower district, the smell hitting them so suddenly that she gagged a little, Darwin turned to Elowen.

"See you around, Farrowspire."

Unable to stop herself, she burst out, "When?"

Darwin just smiled enigmatically and began to walk away, making his way further into the Lower Section. He turned a corner and disappeared into the maze that was the Lower Section. Elowen sighed in frustration.

Not wanting to face Hally just yet with her disappointing news, she decided to head toward Mistress Monige's Home for Foundlings, hoping to hear the rest of what the mistress had wanted to tell her. She weaved her way through the narrow streets until, after almost half an hour of walking, she reached the back of the colourful home where a small courtyard could be found, clothes hanging on lines and flapping in the wind. The back door was open and sitting on the step in front of it were two small girls. They were playing with a black and white kitten and grinned when they saw Elowen approaching.

"Ellie!" they cried, jumping to their feet and rushing toward Elowen. The kitten was dumped unceremoniously on the ground and they threw their arms around Elowen, hugging her tightly.

"Hi, you two." Elowen smiled and patted their backs. One of the girls, who went by the name of Alice, had her black hair tied in pigtails and wore a similar, but smaller dress to Elowen. She stepped back and put her hands on her hips, crossly.

"How come you haven't visited us!" Alice demanded. The other little girl, who was called Fern and wore the same dress, but had her blonde hair hanging loose at her shoulders, nodded vigorously but did not let go of Elowen, instead craning her neck to look up at her.

Elowen smiled. "I missed you, too, Alice."

"Back so soon?" said a melodic voice from the doorway. Elowen looked up, her smile diminishing slightly. Mistress Monige stood in the doorway, arms crossed and a disapproving look on her beautiful face. Elowen bit her lip nervously. The mistress knew she had failed. Elowen did not know how she knew, but that could be the only explanation for her cold greeting.

Mistress Monige rolled her eyes and said, "Come in, child. It's not the end of the world."

Elowen grimaced and replied, "It certainly feels close to it."

"So it would seem," said Monige, sighing and uncrossing her arms. "Come in, come in," she ordered, beckoning them inside. Alice picked up the kitten and skipped after Monige while Fern continued to clutch tightly to Elowen, who was forced to shuffle awkwardly to make her way inside.

The back door led into a large wooden kitchen where a long wooden table and benches stood in the middle. Three more, slightly older, children sat around the table eating from bowls with wooden spoons. They all looked up and smiled as they saw Elowen. Mistress Monige disappeared through the doorway leading into a small pantry to the one side of the kitchen and returned with a bowl of soup that she placed on the table for Elowen. Elowen smiled and, untangling herself from Fern's clutches, she sat down at the table and began to spoon mouthfuls of delicious potato and leek soup into her mouth. She sighed, forgetting, for a second, the test. She barely noticed that the other children, aside from Alice and Fern, had disappeared through the doorway at the front of the kitchen, leaving their empty bowls on the table. A third door stood open to her left where a dark and narrow stairwell could be seen leading up to the next level of the home. Fern sat down beside Elowen and shuffled closer to her as Elowen finished her last spoonful of soup, and Alice began playing with the kitten on the floor as Mistress Monige leaned against the counter, frowning at Elowen.

"What happened?"

Elowen's heart sank as she remembered her failure. "How did find out?" she asked dejectedly.

"I know everything that goes on in this city, child."

"Well, I didn't pass, as you know, and that fault lies with someone named Imogen." Mistress Monige's nostrils flared and her eyes flashed in anger. Surprised, Elowen said, "You know who that is, don't you?"

Monige pursed her lips but didn't answer. Elowen took her silence to mean a 'yes', and so she asked, "Does that mean you know a man by the name of Darwin?

She shrugged nonchalantly. "Everyone knows who Darwin is. He was partly to blame for the War of Fiendish Malice."

"He said he wasn't."

"Of course, he thinks that. No doubt he blames Imogen for that, too." She sighed, her eyes turning misty as she stared at something Elowen couldn't see. "I suppose he wouldn't be wrong."

What the mistress had said nagged Elowen until she finally said, "Mistress Monige... what aren't you telling me?"

Just then, a loud knocking could be heard from the front of the house. Miss Monige glanced toward the kitchen door, her eyes narrowing as though she knew who was at the door. She turned back to Elowen and said, "Please take Fern and Alice upstairs for their sleep. Don't come down until I fetch you."

Alice and Fern, who had also glanced up at the sound of the knocking, looked as though they wanted to protest but at the look on Mistress Monige's face, they seemed to think better of it. Alice picked up the kitten and made her way to the stairwell, while Fern took Elowen's hand and pulled on it gently, leading Elowen to the stairs. As Elowen passed through the doorway, she turned to look back just as Miss Monige disappeared through the door leading to the entrance hall. Elowen closed the door to the stairwell with a snap and she quickly turned to Alice and Fern, who stood behind her in the darkness.

"You two go so long, I'll catch up with you in a minute." She gave them each a little push. They both made their way up quietly, Elowen waiting patiently for them to disappear before turning and kneeling before the keyhole of the door. The Ornette swung forward, almost hitting the door. Elowen grabbed it and held onto it while she listened.

All was quiet for a few seconds, then she heard the kitchen door squeak open and footsteps entering the kitchen. The sound of a kitchen bench being pulled back reached Elowen's ears. Then she heard Miss Monige speak.

"Why have you come? I thought I made myself quite clear last time we spoke that I didn't want to see you or your partner again, and yet I have seen you both on the same day." Monige's voice was dangerously quiet; Elowen had to press her ear hard against the hole to hear.

"Maybe if you'd prepared her better, I wouldn't have to be here," said a familiar voice: Darwin. So they did know each other. "Today should have been a breeze for the girl," Darwin continued, "if you had done what you said you'd do."

"I promised nothing of the sort," Monige replied sharply. "I never agreed to let the child become a Shikari." She spat out the last word with disgust.

"And that's where our problem lay today: in you not playing your part," snapped Darwin. "Your bias against the Shikari will get her killed."

"And your visiting me like this doesn't put her at a greater risk?"

"At least if she were in the Shikari she would be able to defend herself so we wouldn't have to worry about necessary meetings like this one drawing unwanted attention."

"These meetings are *not* necessary," said the mistress angrily. "Elowen is perfectly safe, thanks to me."

They were talking about her. Elowen's heart began to thump so loudly that she worried she might be found out. She took a deep breath and pressed her ear even harder against the keyhole, feeling the edges digging into her flesh uncomfortably.

"How can we trust her to make the right choices if she doesn't know why she needs to make them?"

"You will *not* tell Elowen anything," Monige said forcefully. "Do I make myself plain?"

Elowen could almost hear the smirk in Darwin's next words. "*You* do not tell me what to do, Enchantress." Elowen drew back slightly in confusion, wanting to dig her finger into her ear to make sure she was hearing correctly. "We all agreed she would become a Shikari."

"I agreed to nothing. My plan, which has been going perfectly smoothly, no thanks to you, was always to keep a low profile. Gundrel-"

"That idiot has no say in her future!" Darwin interrupted, raising his voice.

"He has as much a say as you do, which is none at all. Don't you think she will look for Elowen in obvious places like the Shikari and Newids?"

"And you think you don't draw any attention; you stand out like a dragon in a sheep pen. At least my plan prepares Elowen should she come searching for her."

"At least the child doesn't stand out, thanks to *my* strategic plans."

A loud bang of a fist being slammed on the table made Elowen jump and hit the top of her head on the doorknob. She bit her lip as silence followed and she drew back from the door as though expecting it to be opened and her to be found out. But soon she heard the voices continue, softer than before. Elowen quickly brought her ear back to the keyhole.

"Your arrogance will get her killed. She needs to be prepared, for all our sakes. The longer we wait, the more likely it is she will be found and then we are doomed. Do you want what happened to your mistress to happen to Elowen?"

"And you think the Shikari can prepare her?" snarled Miss Monige.

"Certainly better than what you've been doing, which is to say, nothing at all. What do you think she will say if she hears her daughter knows nothing, thanks to you?"

"Thanks to me, she is alive and independent and well-hidden. And she knows enough to survive, again, thanks to me."

"Well, congratulations. You must be so proud. At least if she dies she can say she knows how to live by herself."

Elowen heard footsteps and a sharp *slap* echoed through the kitchen. Her legs were beginning to protest from crouching for so long, but she dared not move; she was so enraptured by what she was hearing. She just wished she could make sense of it all.

"You are not her mother, Imogen," she heard Darwin say, sharply.

Imogen, Elowen mouthed, confused. Who was Imogen? Just then, she heard another bang of what sounded like a door being opened and another voice sounded through the kitchen.

"That's enough, you two!" said the voice.

"Gavin!" said Darwin, shock coating his words. "What are you doing here?"

"I'm here because I knew you would come here, Darwin."

"Get out, both of you," snapped the mistress. "Neither of you should be here."

"I'm afraid the time for secrecy is over, Imogen," said Gavin. "The child must join the Shikari."

"How," snarled Darwin, "When this Enchantress has been doing everything in her power to prevent that from happening. It's her fault the girl failed the test."

"No, she didn't," said Gavin quietly.

There was a pause, then, "Excuse me?" said Darwin.

"She passed the first test."

Elowen blinked rapidly, shock causing her to gasp, then, for the second time, she jumped in fright, hitting her head against the doorknob again, as a voice said loudly behind her, "Are you coming, Elowen?"

Alice and Fern stood on the stairs looking at her curiously. Elowen tried to gesture for them to be quiet and go, but just as she put her finger to her lips, the door to the kitchen opened and she fell back onto the kitchen floor, the sudden light making her blink up stupidly.

Above her stood three people: Darwin in the middle, Gavin to his left, and Mistress Monige to his right. Darwin's eyebrow was raised in amusement, while Mistress Monige looked most unsurprised by Elowen's appearance. Gavin had his dagger out, pointing at Elowen.

Then he smiled grimly, sheathing his dagger, and said, "Good afternoon, again, Miss Farrowspire. I think it's time we talked.

Chapter 6

Troubling Tales

As day turned to starry night, a party of four could be found at the dark corner table in the Dastardly Boar, a table known to the many frequenters of the alehouse as the place where misdeeds were planned. Assassins and thieves usually sat there where shadows crawled along the walls and whispers buried themselves in the wood, never to be heard again. The patrons of the alehouse were accustomed to these kinds of people, but they were not used to the four people who currently sat in the corner of the dimly lit room. One so easily recognizable by her dark beauty was the Mistress Monige of the Foundling Home. On her left sat two men known to the patrons as Shikari and on her right sat the unusual girl who went by the name Elowen.

Elowen, Mistress Monige, whose real name Elowen had determined was Imogen, Darwin and Gavin had decided to relocate to the Dastardly Boar to have their talk. The group huddled around the small and low corner table that carried two tankards of ale and two goblets of mead. They all looked disproportionately big on their stools and sat uncomfortably close together. Their lack of proximity to the other tables, as well as the large number of patrons of the alehouse who, in their drunken state, were talking and laughing loudly, made it the perfect place to have a private discussion and not be overheard. At the front of the house was a bard called Yemik who drew attention away from the table with his merry, catchy song:

A fair maiden, men would say.
But trust naught for to this day
Nary a man did she ever love
Only Kervin the Newidly dove.
Oh, but as fate would have it:
The Newid did admit,
"'Tis a union much too foul!"
And now she's all but scowls.

Cheers and laughter followed the jolly song's end, patrons clapping and stomping their feet, all except the group at the corner table.

The group at this table sat in a deathly silence in the semi-darkness of the corner. Imogen's arms and legs were crossed and a scowl pulled at her face for she did not appreciate being pulled away from her home and having to put the older children in charge. She was rarely seen outside her home for foundlings. She had, however, been given the choice: stay home and not be part of their conversation, or come with and help them fill Elowen in. She had chosen the latter, not trusting the men to share the right information.

Darwin looked quite at home in the Dastardly Boar, and he took a sip of his ale, smacking his lips. He glanced around the room, seemed to see someone he knew and waved, and Elowen, following his gaze, was shocked to see Hally wave back at him. Her friend, dressed in a loose barmaid dress, noticed Elowen beside Darwin, and quickly turned and busied herself with cleaning an already-clean table.

Gavin finally put down his tankard of ale that he had downed in one go, wiped his lips and sighed contentedly, before glancing around surreptitiously to ensure they would, indeed, not be overheard. When he opened his mouth to speak, however, he was interrupted by a curious Elowen, who leaned across the table toward Darwin.

"How do you know Hally," she demanded, narrowing her eyes at Darwin. Gavin closed his mouth, looking confused, then gazed at

Darwin questioningly. The Mistress just picked up her mead and took a delicate sip from it.

Darwin, surprised, replied, "Well, I had to get someone to watch over you and she was up for the job."

"What?" said Elowen, confused, and reached for her mead. "Wait, Hally is keeping watch over me?"

"Yes. She gives me regular updates on your safety. And she's a damn good barmaid, though don't tell her I said that. She normally serves me when I come here for a drink... in disguise, of course," he finished quickly, glancing at Gavin guiltily. Gavin turned slightly red and his moustache bristled angrily; Darwin had been banned from many of the taverns in the city, including this one, due to his knack of starting brawls. Bartholomew had made an exception for tonight.

Gavin stared a Hally, and then realisation seemed to hit and he opened and closed his mouth several times like a fish, before finally saying, "Wait, is that Halina?" When Darwin nodded, Gavin's eyebrows rose and he continued, "She looks so different. I didn't recognise her. When did she start working here?"

Darwin shrugged and said, rather smugly, "As soon as Elowen moved here, and, once it had become clear that Imogen wasn't doing her part to encourage Elowen to enter the tournament, I thought asking another person to help convince her was our best course of action. And who better than another Shikari? Hally was only too happy to assist."

Elowen, who had been sipping on her mead, choked, spluttering and messing mead down the front of her dress. "Hally is a Shikari?" she asked, a little loudly. Darwin ignored her question as he had just noticed Imogen rolling her eyes at him.

"Why do you think I told her to rent here," Imogen said drolly, "and why was it so easy for her to do so? Bartholomew was hired by me to protect her."

Darwin snorted. "You think an ordinary man is better than a Shikari?"

"I know for a fact he is as good as." retorted Imogen.

Gavin wasn't listening but was instead trying to get Hally's attention to get her to join them. When she finally glanced in their direction, she nodded and made her way to their table. She grabbed a stool behind a drunken man standing yelling for more ale, who then took a seat, promptly falling to his backside and earning jeers and laughter from his peers. Hally placed the chair between Darwin and Gavin and smiled at Elowen as she took a seat. Her smile faltered at the look on Elowen's face.

"Shikari?!" mouthed Elowen, narrowing her eyes, then looking away when Darwin cried, "Halina!" and gave her a hearty punch on the shoulder. He looked over to where Bartholomew stood behind the counter and shouted over the din, "Barty! Bring us another ale!" Then he turned back to Hally and said, "Fantastic job you did, convincing Elowen to enter the tournament. How'd you do it?"

Bartholomew arrived with another tankard of ale for Hally then made his way back to the bar.

Hally shrugged at Darwin, taking a sip of ale, and said, "Well, she needed a partner and I was happy to join her party. We are friends, after all, aren't we, El?"

"Are we?" snapped Elowen. "I thought friendship was based on honesty." Elowen looked away, feeling somewhat guilty about her harshness.

Hally sighed and, grabbing Elowen's hand tightly, forcing Elowen to look at her, she said, "We are friends, El. Don't doubt that. I care for you more than you know. I'm sorry I didn't tell you, I am, but I had sworn not to say a word."

Darwin nodded, taking another swig of ale. "She did." Then he looked at Imogen and said, "See, I kept our agreement - Elowen knew nothing."

Imogen was silent as she put down her mead. Then she said, sighing, "What are you thinking of, then? Letting her die in this damn tournament of yours?"

"At least I am doing something to help her," snarled Darwin.

Imogen slammed her hands down on the table, rising slightly, and said, "And what do you think I've been doing for her up until now? Everything she knows is because of me."

Gavin put up his hands then and everyone looked at him, Elowen somewhat reluctantly.

"Enough, you two. The time has come for her to know about her past so that she can be prepared for her future, now that she has succeeded in passing the first test."

Hally let out a whoop while Darwin grinned at Elowen. Imogen pursed her lips, sitting back down.

"But I didn't," said Elowen quietly before she could stop herself. They all turned to look at her. She took another sip of mead, feeling suddenly self-conscious, and continued, "That leader, Buze - he said I had failed."

"Buze is a bloody idiot," replied Gavin, as though that settled the matter. When Elowen continued to look unconvinced he sighed and said, "Buze believes he is better than everyone, and, as you are a Lower, you are like an insect that needs to be squished to him. In his mind, he can use his power as leader of the Shikari Academy to choose who can enter, whether they pass or not."

"Idiot," Darwin agreed, spitting on the ground in anger, narrowly missing Hally who looked at him in disgust, then he said, "So he lied to Elowen?"

Gavin nodded and took a swig from his tankard before realising it was finished. Then he said to Elowen, "You must have seen how surprised I was when he told you your verdict? No? Well, I was. You answered most of the questions correctly, clever girl. But it seems the other leaders had all silently agreed that you were not worth allowing to enter the tournament, even when I protested after you had left. I eventually had to go to Master Gimrad when they refused to back down."

"Master Gimrad overruled Buze?" Hally said, her eyebrows rising so high they hid behind her fringe. "Why?"

"Master Gimrad was the one I contacted," said Imogen, quietly, her eyes going misty.

"Eh?" asked Darwin, frowning, confused at the interruption.

"Twenty years ago, when I hired the Shikari to get Elowen out of Milas."

Elowen glanced at Imogen, surprised. She had never heard this story before. She held her breath, eager to hear more, but was disappointed when Hally interjected.

"You contacted the Master of the Shikari?" said Hally, impressed. Imogen nodded.

"Well, he wasn't the Master back then," Gavin corrected. "He was just the head of fieldwork and missions. Anyway, I believe only he and I knew of the mission in its entirety, besides Imogen and Gundrel, so of course I went to the Master for help now."

"He contacted me recently, you know," said Imogen softly.

"Who, Gimrad?" asked Gavin, confused.

"No, Gundrel."

"What did he want?" asked Gavin calmly, though his moustache bristled slightly.

"Elowen."

"Well, he can't have her," said Darwin loudly. "She is going to be a Shikari." Hally gave another cheer and Darwin banged his tankard down in enthusiasm, causing the contents to splash across the table.

Imogen bristled. "I believe it is my right to decide that. Gundrel seemed to understand that when he asked me to speak to her."

"She is not a Newid!" snarled Darwin.

"She is more Newid than she is human," spat Imogen. "I decide what she does!"

"Says who?!"

"Her mother!" Imogen snapped, rising slightly, an aura of power surrounding her and making the rest of the group shrink back slightly.

There was an awkward silence after that. Elowen glanced from one person to the next, wanting to say something but struggling to find the right words, or, in fact, the right question. Eventually, Hally said, after glancing at Elowen, "Excuse me, but I believe Elowen has more right than anyone else to decide her fate now that she is of age."

Elowen looked at Hally in surprised gratitude and then found everyone staring at her, as though they had only just remembered she was there. A small headache was starting to form at Elowen's temples and she rubbed them gently before saying, "Why is it so important that I enter the Tournament?"

"So that you can learn to defend yourself and be prepared," said Gavin

"For what," she pressed.

"For her... the queen," said Imogen softly. It was the first time Elowen had ever seen a look of fear on her face, mirrored by the other members.

A shiver that had nothing to do with the air around her ran up Elowen's spine and she stared around the group before saying, "Why me, a Lower? I'm nobody."

"You are not nobody," snapped Imogen, bristling in anger. "Don't you ever believe that. Not after all your mother and father did to protect you. After what we did."

Elowen frowned and said quickly, "I still don't understand. If they cared so much for me, where are they now? I've never seen or heard from them."

"Your mother and father are very important to their people-"

"But I'm not important to them?" snapped Elowen.

Imogen held up her delicate hand, and then she said, "I'm sorry, Elowen. I forget how much you do not know. Your mother and father are critical in their family and tribe. Your mom was my mistress in Milas-"

"The Coven of the Dark's village?" Elowen interrupted, surprised.

"Yes, she is an Enchantress, like me."

"You're a Coven of the Dark Enchantress?" Elowen gasped shifting ever so slightly away from Imogen.

"As are you, child," she snapped angrily, narrowing her eyes at Elowen's movement.

"Half-Enchantress," corrected Darwin, earning a scowl from Imogen. "Well, it's true." He turned to Elowen and said, "Your father is one of the Raethenian princes from Mount Aarde, though he lives in Rostefen."

Elowen shook her head. She looked nothing like Imogen, and, according to the stories she'd heard of Newids, she had none of their characteristics, either.

"There must be some mistake," Elowen said, "I'm just a foundling from the Lower Section. It's more likely my parents were too poor to keep me or they died from... the Genja Flu, or something. Why would a prince or Enchantress just abandon me? If they were so important and powerful, why couldn't they protect me themselves?"

Hally stared at Elowen with a mixture of pity and frustration. She shook her head and said, "I still can't believe she knows nothing."

Elowen bristled, wanting to say that she knew things and wasn't some fool. But her head was swarming with questions and it took everything to focus her thoughts and say, "Where are they now? Do they not care what is happening to me?" She felt a strange, prickling sensation behind her eyes; she was surprised by how much emotion that one question had elicited.

Imogen patted her dress, smoothing out invisible wrinkles, and replied, "We don't know. After the War of Fiendish Malice began, we lost touch with the Enchantresses and Newids. The last time we had any contact was the day you were born."

"The war started after I was born?" asked Elowen.

"The war started because you were born," Hally chirped quietly.

Elowen looked from one person to the next, thinking they were telling some sort of joke. When no one laughed, she giggled nervously and said, disbelievingly, "I started the war?"

Imogen shrugged and said, "I suppose it didn't help that we kidnapped you."

"Yeah, the Enchantresses were not happy that you had been taken away," said Gavin. "Luckily they blamed the Newids at first until the Shikari's involvement became known. By that time we were long gone."

"But why me?" whispered Elowen.

"There was a prophecy made about you," replied Gavin.

"No," said Imogen suddenly, "she cannot know her own prophecy. It is bad luck."

Darwin snorted into his drink, earning another repulsed look from Hally. "You Enchantresses are always so superstitious."

"It is not superstition, boy," Imogen snarled. "It is very old magic, the kind you could never dream of understanding. Do not try to educate me on things you have no experience in."

"Calm down, Imogen," said Gavin quietly.

Elowen bit her fingernail, feeling confused and overwhelmed. She wanted, needed, to know more, but they had already moved onto another topic - the Tournament.

"You were supposed to prepare her," Darwin was saying, to which Imogen replied, "She passed, didn't she?"

Elowen placed her hand down loudly on the table and said, "Stop!" Her headache was slowly starting to creep to the middle of her forehead. They all turned to look at her, mostly with a frustrated or pitying look, making Elowen feel more irritable.

"We have been here for almost an hour and I know little more than I did when we got here. Someone had better fill me in or, so help me, I will not do the tournament."

Gavin chuckled. "She has spirit. All right, girl, I will tell you as much as I know." He paused for a while, his face screwed up in concentration as he thought back. "For me," he began, slowly, "this all started on an abnormally cold spring night twenty years ago."

There was silence around the table as everyone began to listen closely to what Gavin said. The shouts and laughter of the drunken men in the Dastardly Boar were soon forgotten as they all became engrossed in what he was saying.

"Gimrad," Gavin continued, keeping his voice low, "the field and missions leader, called me in to discuss a mission he would be sending Darwin and me on the next day.

"He had received a raven with a very peculiar message. Apparently, the Coven of the Dark Queen's daughter was expecting a child and this daughter's lady's maid," he gestured at Imogen, "believed that this baby would need to be removed from Milas as quickly as possible. According to Imogen, there was a prophecy made that suggested that the lineage of the child, as well as the magic poured into her in the womb, would make her the Enchantress's greatest weapon. This needed to be avoided at all costs.

A loud bang as a man fell off his stool close to the party's table caused the tavern to burst into rowdy laughter and cheers. Hally rolled her eyes but Gavin just continued as though there had been no interruption.

"I'm afraid to say neither Gimrad nor I put much store in the message, though we did agree that, should it prove to be true, then we would have made a grave mistake in not going to the village to look into it. We also agreed that should it be true, we would need to kill the baby then and there, and any Enchantresses that got in our way."

Elowen's eyes widened and she swallowed nervously. They were speaking about killing her. Yet, she reminded herself, she was still here so they couldn't still wish her dead... could they?

"When we arrived, we soon found we were not the only ones who had been told of the child's imminent birth. The Newids were told, too, and they all started arriving sometime after we did. First to arrive, the Traewen Newids of the coastal village Quana followed shortly after by the Reifen Newids of the desert village Woestyn. A week later, the last three tribes - the Raethen Newids of Mount Aarde, the Rostefen Newids of the Glyphwood Forest, and the Iranen Newids of Lahntberg - set up their camps as far away from each other as possible. Lucky for us, too, or we might have run into each other." Gavin proceeded to tell her how they had met with Imogen and a Newid called Gundrel and then made their way to the place where Elowen's mother was giving birth. "We took the baby, you, as per your mother's request, and agreed to get you as far away as possible."

"Why were the other Newids there," asked Elowen, though having a feeling she already knew the answer.

Imogen answered this time. "For you. The Newids had been invited by the queen to celebrate your birth. Or, at least, that's what they had been told would happen."

"What do you mean?" Hally whispered, enthralled.

Imogen sighed and replied, "You have to understand that the Coven of the Dark Enchantresses have never been known for their practices in 'safe' magic. We have always pushed the boundaries, the idea of what is right and good is somewhat unimportant. Not all the Coven of the Dark Enchantresses are like that, but most are, meaning that those who do not agree with our practices get killed, and sacrificed as a means to gain more magical power."

"See," Elowen heard Darwin whisper to Gavin, "I told you you gain some of their powers when you kill them." Gavin rolled his eyes and sighed.

Imogen nodded and said, "If you know the right spell, you can take that magic for yourself. That is why the queen is so strong. Anyway, the same spell that takes the magic of the sacrificed Coven of the Darks was going to be used on the Newids, though they had no idea. By spilling their blood on the eve of your birth, you might gain some of their powers. Or, at least, that's the theory. It's never been done before."

"Wait," said Darwin suddenly, his eyes wide, "that's why the war started, isn't it? Not because they thought the Newids had kidnapped Elowen, but because they killed all those Newids for their powers?"

"Yes... and no," replied Imogen, looking down as she smoothed out her dress again unnecessarily. "I believe the queen did believe they had taken Elowen. I believe she just used that as an excuse to continue to carry out the sacrifice. It was to her benefit as the other Enchantress families had no idea about this spell that was cast - they believed the Newids had been killed for kidnapping the child. This is why they happily joined forces with the Coven of the Dark, something that has not happened in centuries. The Newids, of course, knew their ambassadors had been innocent and so their tribes joined forces to fight the Enchantresses. It was only recently that the Enchantresses somehow found out the Shikari had been involved and the war was then brought to the humans' doorstep."

Silence followed her words and the group sat contemplating what she had said. But for Elowen, several things still did not make sense and she was itching to ask the most important one.

"Why didn't you kill me," she said, her heart hammering as though expecting them to be suddenly reminded that they still needed to do that.

Gavin gave her a bitter smile and said, "We tried."

Elowen gulped and shifted away slightly. He shook his head and gazed at her sadly.

"I'm sorry, Elowen. We were following orders. But it turned out a spell had been placed on us that prevented us from killing you."

"A spell? Who...."

"Me," said Imogen quietly. She had a look of deep sadness on her face as she went on, "Your mother made me promise to protect you and I knew the Shikari would want you dead. Eventually, we came to an agreement and the four of us made it our mission to protect you from that moment on."

"Then what does any of this have to do with the tournament?" asked Elowen warily.

"You need to be prepared if the queen comes looking for you," replied Gavin gently. "You've been protected in this city your whole life, but out there, the war that started when you were born continues to this day. I'm not saying you need to choose a side now, but, when you do, you should be prepared."

Elowen nodded slowly, then said, "Where is my mother now?"

Pain flashed across Imogen's face. "She's trapped in Milas, so my sources tell me. Your grandmother, no doubt, figured out your mother had organised everything behind her back and has spent the last twenty years searching for you while punishing your mother."

"So she's still alive?" asked Elowen hopefully.

Imogen nodded. "But I don't expect her to be the same as she was the day I left her. Our means of torture are... grotesque." She looked away, her eyes flashing in anger.

"And my father?"

Gavin answered this time, looking at Imogen carefully. "Alive, if Gundrel is trying to get to you."

"Gundrel?"

"A Newid who works for your father and was tasked with ensuring your safe removal from Milas. If Imogen says he's contacted her, that means your father wishes you to join him."

Elowen's eyes widened and her heart lifted. "But that's great! I can go to him and-"

"No."

Darwin, Gavin and Imogen had all interrupted her at the same time, all looking disturbed.

"Do not trust them, Elowen," said Imogen. "He might be your father, but Newids are not known to be the caring or nurturing type."

"But-"

"Elowen, trust us," said Gavin, looking her dead in the eyes. "You are better off learning to protect yourself with us. Please." He looked so serious and worried, that Elowen fell silent, though she was still thinking about her father and mother. It made more sense to her to find her family than to enter some tournament to join a guild that would train her in fighting magical creatures, but she said nothing.

The group became aware of the sudden drop in noise in the tavern and all five members glanced around curiously. The tavern had slowly but surely begun to empty as they had talked and the last few patrons hung onto their tables in a drunken state, listening to the end of Yemik's slow, sad dirge:

<blockquote>
Oh, sad indeed, was the death of Sir Halbirs

And his merry band of adventurers.

And though no one comprehends,

The party of the five friends

were never seen again.
</blockquote>

One of the patrons burst into tears and howled, gulping out a teary, "Too true!"

"That's my cue," sighed Hally, and she stood up and stretched. She gave Elowen a small smile and said, "See you tomorrow, El." Then she made her way to the tearful man and helped him to his feet, leading him toward the door of the alehouse.

Imogen stood, too, and said, "I had best be going before the home turns to shambles." She made her way after Hally and disappeared into the night.

Darwin and Gavin stared at Elowen, until she eventually said, "Now what?"

"Now the fun begins," grinned Darwin, rubbing his hands together.

Gavin nodded, smiling, and said, "Tomorrow, we'll get you kitted out for your stay at Pamor and the Tournament that will follow. Then, after that, your training begins. We'll head out with the other Tournament participants and their party members on horseback and go to Pamor Tower. Are you ready, Farrowspire?

Elowen didn't answer, but later that evening, as she got into her nightgown, the Ornette in full view, blinking up at her every so often, and into bed, she thought about all that had been said and pondered on Gavin's question.

"Yes," she finally answered to the empty room. "I'm ready."

And into the darkness came a whisper as she drifted off to sleep. *Good. You will need to be, Elowen Farrowspire.*

Chapter 7

Preparations

The far-off crow of a rooster called in the start of a new and blustery day in the city of Illfang. The wind howled, rattling the windows of the room above the tavern as though desperate to get in, while the sun, peeking over the many uneven rooftops, streamed in to chase away the chill from the night before. From the street below the lodgings, the sounds of early morning activity filtered into the silent room where Elowen, dressed in her usual clothes, could be found perched on the edge of her seat beside the window. She tapped her foot impatiently while squinting through the glare of the sun, her eyes shifting to the road below. Suddenly, as if having seen something, Elowen stood up, put on her coat, and headed out the door of the dormitory.

She had made it halfway down the stairs when she heard the door to the tavern squeak open. She hurried eagerly down the remaining stairs, taking the last five at a jump and landing at the bottom with a loud thump. Darwin stood silhouetted in the entrance to the almost empty tavern and he grinned when he saw Elowen.

"Nice to see I don't have to come wake you," he said. He was wearing a similar outfit to the one he had been wearing the day before and he adjusted his Shikari badge before making his way inside. There were three other people in the tavern, seated together at the same table and talking in hushed tones. They looked around briefly at Elowen and Darwin, then continued with their conversation.

"Oh, I thought we were leaving," said Elowen, slightly disappointed as the door shut behind Darwin.

"Eager, are you?" he laughed, sitting down at a table close to the bar. "I thought we'd get some breakfast."

"Now?" Elowen said, impatiently. She did not feel remotely hungry.

Darwin laughed and held up his hands. "Relax, El. Breakfast first." He paused suddenly as he looked her over, noting her dress and worn coat. Frowning, he said, "You're wearing that today?"

Elowen looked down at herself and shrugged. "What's wrong with it? That's all I have."

"Well, that won't do. We'll be going into the Upper Section today, so you'll need to blend in better than that, and that dress shouts 'poverty.'"

Elowen scowled, "Excuse me, but I'll have you know this dress is from Mistress Monige -"

"Imogen."

"Imogen, and she would be most displeased to hear you say that." She sniffed, brushing off some dust from her coat.

Darwin grinned and said, "Well, I won't tell her if you don't. Calm down," he said, earning a deeper scowl from Elowen. "All I meant was that the Uppers will know you're not one of them and it will make the day all the more tedious, which seems unnecessary. We'll ask Hally if she has something for you."

He nodded to himself and then looked over at the kitchen door as it opened and Bartholomew appeared in the doorway. "Ah, Bart! Two breakfasts please."

Elowen sat down next to Darwin as Bartholomew disappeared into the kitchen again. They heard banging and scraping and he soon returned with two bowls of meaty stew and watered-down wine. Darwin looked slightly disappointed but dug in anyway. Elowen stared at her stew for a minute before taking a few spoonfuls.

Darwin leaned over to Elowen and said, stew dripping from the corner of his mouth, "I was hoping for eggs or bacon."

Elowen rolled her eyes and replied, "This is the Lower Section, Darwin. Stew is the best you're going to get." She took another spoonful and then pushed the bowl away, feeling queasy.

"You're going to love Pamor, then. I gained five pounds last time I went there, the food is so good."

A dozen questions went through Elowen's mind. She picked one and asked, "What will the first day of training entail at Pamor?"

"Well, it will mostly be an introduction to what you might need for the Tournament and you will be allowed to choose which parts of the training you will focus on."

"Any advice?" she asked, nervously.

He paused, a spoonful of stew halfway to his mouth. "Maybe focus on not drawing too much attention to yourself. The less of a threat you are, the better."

Elowen frowned. "Shouldn't you be telling me to do my best?"

Darwin laughed, but as he was about to answer, the door to the stairs opened and Hally appeared, wearing a poofy, bright purple dress with capped sleeves and bonnet to match, her hair curled into a bun below the brim. Elowen stifled a giggle as Hally shoved herself through the narrow doorway, nearly overbalancing as she landed.

"Well, you look much better prepared than Elowen," said Darwin approvingly, pushing his empty bowl of stew away.

"Thanks!" Hally answered brightly, making her way around the bar to sit beside them. She spent a good minute trying to sit on the bar stool, the hoop in her dress bending this way and that, until she eventually gave up, squeezed between two stools and leaned against the bar. She winked at Elowen as though aware Elowen was trying not to laugh.

Elowen began, "You look... er...."

"Gorgeous? Rich? Amiable?"

"Ridiculous," snorted Elowen.

Hally stuck out her tongue and said, "And what do you think you'll be wearing? "

The smile was wiped off Elowen's face. Hally smirked. "Exactly." She brushed away an invisible piece of dust from her shoulder and proceeded to pull on satin gloves. "I've left a dress for you on your bed, El."

Elowen sighed and stood slowly from her stool. "I guess I'll be back in a second." She went round the back of the bar and disappeared up the stairs.

"I'd better go help her." Hally smiled and followed Elowen up the stairs with much rustling of material and tapping of her heels.

Darwin waited patiently at the bar for what felt like an age. By the time the stairway creaked to announce their arrival, Darwin had already finished another bowl of stew. Down the stairs came Hally, followed some distance behind by a very unsteady Elowen. Elowen now wore a periwinkle blue dress of equally sizeable proportions, pretty lace adorning the bottom and top of the dress, with a similar-looking blue bonnet, which she pulled at in discomfort.

"Stop fiddling," muttered Hally, grinning.

"It's pinching in all the wrong places and I can barely breathe." Elowen gave a great gasp as though to emphasise her point.

"Buck up," said Darwin, standing from his stool and giving a small belch. "It's only for today."

Elowen glared at Darwin and Hally gave him a serious look.

"Perhaps you should wear my other dress and we'll tell you to buck up when you complain," said Hally, raising her eyebrow at Darwin. He raised his hands in defeat and replied, "Let's just get going then. Oh, and your money." He tossed a purse to Elowen, who caught it deftly, grinning in delight and anticipation at the weight of it. "From Mistress Monige. One hundred and fifty gold pieces."

It had taken most of the morning to finish getting ready for the trip to the Upper Section, so, by the time they exited the Dastardly Boar, the sun beat down on them from its apex almost as strongly as the wind, which howled through the streets, bringing with it the smell of squalor. Hally and Elowen grasped their bonnets as the wind tugged at their outfits and they stepped down into the dust of the street, Darwin following closely behind.

The walk to the portcullis separating the two sections was an annoyingly arduous one as the girls had to walk slowly, holding up their dresses, to avoid getting too much dirt on them. Darwin made sure to sigh at just the right times to make his impatience known until Hally eventually hit him over the head with her small, drawstring bag.

"If you don't stop complaining, Darwin," started Hally, giving him a dark look, "I will make you regret having me as your first champion."

Darwin rolled his eyes, though said nothing as they passed into the shadow of the great portcullis separating the Lower and Upper Section. The guards, who, Elowen noted, were the same guards who had refused to let her pass the day before, nodded at Darwin and bowed at Hally and Elowen. Elowen had the sudden urge to punch them in the face but resisted as the three passed through into the start of the Upper Section, which had reached its busiest time.

"So, where are we going first?" asked Elowen as they headed up the main street, approaching the first set of stairs.

"First we get you your clothes," said Darwin, turning down the avenue to the left of the stairs. Lined with many tall poplar trees, the road stretching ahead of them was teeming with people and the three of them were jostled by the many Uppers heading to and from the main shopping district at the end of the long avenue.

Elowen felt a sense of relief as she saw that the many women walking the street were wearing similar clothing to her and Hally of many different colours so that the road looked alive, like a river of colour. She had never felt more grateful to be wearing such a hideously uncomfortable outfit.

The shopping district at the end of the avenue was the biggest Elowen had ever seen. It stretched ahead of them with thousands of different stalls not unlike the Lower Section market, though different in its quaint building style. Elowen couldn't help the thrill that rushed through her - she had always loved going to the market, but this was on another level entirely.

She started forward eagerly but came to a sudden stop when Hally grabbed her arm.

"What?" Elowen said irritably. She wanted to explore and spend money like she had never had the chance to do before.

"I think we need a plan, and a place to meet in case we get split up." Hally bit her lip in worry. She looked the exact opposite of Elowen - eager to leave as soon as possible and not at all excited to explore.

"We'll meet back here in case we get lost," said Darwin placatingly, "Though we should be fine. I say we start with her clothes, then get her weapons, then organise her ride and perhaps get something to eat before we leave. How does that sound?"

And that is exactly what they did, though if Darwin had thought it would be an easy, straightforward day of shopping, he would have been wrong. Elowen, it turned out, was rather good at spending money, which, as Hally commented several times, was surprising in itself as Elowen had never had very much of it to have had much practice doing so. But spend the money, she did, at many, many stalls over the day, much to Hally and Darwin's dismay.

All the stalls in the shopping district were separated along three parallel roads that ran between two waterways carving their way through the Upper Section. The stalls were built so close together that the wares of each almost tumbled over each other. It was a cacophony of sounds and varying sights and smells and colours, and stalls rose at different levels, joined by thin bridges on the higher levels. The roofs were of many different colours, though the walls were all pale yellowish stone. The shop faces were all open and through each could be seen the labourers at work at the back making their wares.

They spent a good hour browsing different stalls, like the bookstore where Elowen spent far too much time browsing books and scrolls ("Can I buy just one spell scroll, please," Elowen whined to Darwin), the food store for ration packs ("This is boring," moaned Elowen), magical items store where she was most tempted to buy a ring of mind shielding and a wand of wonder ("You don't even know what that is!" cried Darwin), a familiars store ("They're more of a nuisance than anything," explained Hally), though their first real stop was a stall called Borron Leatherworks selling leather armour, where they bought a smooth, rich-looking black one and a warm brown one, both made up of a hood, helms, leg and chest armour, leather boots and gloves, and gauntlets.

"The breastplate and shoulder protectors of this armour," said the leatherworker as they looked at it, "are made of leather that has been stiffened by being boiled in oil. The rest of the armour is made of softer and more flexible materials."

Elowen spent extra on a third set with retractable daggers, much to Darwin's disapproval ("When are you likely to use that?"). Hally bought a large, but comfortable-looking backpack, which, she said, would carry their gear through the rest of the shopping district and the Marasae Labyrinth.

They, then, stopped at the local blacksmith Steelfire to buy some iron tools, followed by a visit to the armoury Obsidian for weapons, then a trip to the apothecary Spellbound to buy healing potions ("It costs how much?!" cried Elowen.) and finally the stables to buy riding gear for the horses that had been chosen for her and Hally, which they left at the stable to be gathered the next morning.

By the time they came out of the stables, the sky had beautiful pink and purple hues painted across it signalling the close of another day.

They made their way home munching on pies they had bought from the pastry shop at the far end of the district.

When they eventually arrived home, stars spotted the inky black sky in a glorious display. Hally and Elowen said goodbye to Darwin and made their way upstairs to Elowen's room, emptying the bag and dumping their purchases on the bed to be checked and sorted.

Hally sat down at the desk, pulled out a piece of parchment and quill and ink from its drawer, and began making an inventory. All was silent in the room as she wrote. Eventually, she looked up at Elowen, who had been admiring her purchases one by one. She handed the parchment over to Elowen to check.

Elowen glanced at the paper and stifled a giggle.

"What's so funny," demanded Hally.

"It's so... perfect." sniggered Elowen, placing the parchment on the bed in the light from the main lamp. She glanced through it quickly.

It was a list showing the items they would take with them as well as the weight, quantity and cost. Elowen was impressed with the elegance and detail of it and smiled slightly as she went through each item, calculating the total weight that Hally would have to carry through the maze.

Name	Weight	Quantity	Cost
Arrows	1lb	20	1GP
Clothes	3lb	2	50SP
Leather Armour	10lb	3	10GP
Dagger	1lb	2	4GP
Scimitar	3lb	1	25GP
Longbow	2lb	1	50GP
Lockpicking tools	1lb	1	25GP
Crowbar	5lb	1	2GP
Piton	2.5lb	10	50SP
Hooded lantern	2lb	1	5GP
Rations	10lb	5	2GP
Hempen rope (50 feet)	10lb	1	1GP
Tinderbox	1lb	1	5SP
Waterskin	5lb	1	20SP

"The pack will be about nineteen pounds which should be fine," said Hally thoughtfully. "The rest you will have to carry if we are to move with speed."

"What are lockpicking tools?" asked Elowen, curiously, pointing at the list.

"That's the small mirror mounted on a metal handle," replied Hally, counting off her fingers, "the set of narrow-bladed scissors, and the pair of pliers that we bought. You know, just in case we need it."

"Well, that's one thing I'll need to learn at Pamor."

Hally smiled. "I'll teach you if you'd like."

"Seems you have a lot to teach me. I still can't believe you have been a Shikari this whole time and never told me."

Hally sighed. "Put yourself in my shoes, El. I was sworn not to tell you. What would you have done?

"It's just that, how can I trust you, trust what we are? Are we even real friends?" Elowen shook her head and bit her lip. Part of her wished she had never found out.

Hally grabbed her shoulders, forcing Elowen to look at her, and said, "My job was to watch over you and I was not to let you find out I'm a Shikari. That means our friendship is something special that just happened and shouldn't that in itself be celebrated?"

Elowen looked away and didn't answer. She didn't know if she was being unfair, but the most important part of friendship is trust and there could be none between them now.

Hally sighed again, though this time more irritably. "Well, you let me know at your leisure, Elowen. See you at the stables tomorrow."

Hally stormed out of the room, her long dark hair flying behind her, and the door shut with a bang.

Elowen stared after Hally for a few seconds, guilt clawing at her heart. She stared at the door, willing Hally to come back, but it remained closed and silent.

Well, that could have gone better.

Elowen jumped backwards, hitting her head against the wall with a loud bang. Bits of dirt and dust rained down on her and she sneezed before glancing widely about the room. Had she imagined that voice, such a cold, calculating voice that brought shivers up and down her spine?

No, you did not.

The voice was loud enough that it did not feel like it was in her head. In fact, it felt as though there was another person in her room. She stood up suddenly and whipped around, squinting through the dark and saw... nothing. She checked under the bed, took several large steps around the room to determine if there was someone using invisibility potions, then, after no success in getting any more answers, she lay on the bed on her side and pondered the possibility of either having gone mad or that she was just tired.

You are neither.

And that's when she saw it. Hidden between her arms and amongst the many frills of her dress, the Ornette glowed brightly, its eye winking. Elowen took up the pendant and stared at it, watching it blink and glow red.

"You?" whispered Elowen, feeling stupid.

Me.

Elowen almost dropped the Ornette in fright, but held it firm and stared at it in wonder. A small part of her screamed for her to throw it away, but she resisted out of curiosity.

Good, Elowen. Good.

"What are you?"

I am the Ornette and you will listen... or die.

Chapter 8

The Ornette

Elowen reached up to remove the necklace, but it would not budge. No matter which way she pulled it, it remained around her neck, pressed against her skin, cold and unyielding. She began hyperventilating, clawing at it, but the eye just blinked up at her, unconcerned and uncaring.

The Dark Enchantress should have told you that you wouldn't be able to remove me.

The voice echoed around the room, or perhaps in her head - she couldn't be sure.

"What are you?" she whispered again, fear coating her words.

You are afraid. I cannot harm you, but fail to heed my words and you will die by the hands of those from whom I am sworn to protect you.

Elowen frowned, not sure whether to believe the voice. She reached for one of the daggers on the bed beside her, and, bending forward, lay the pendant on the table and raised the dagger, ready to strike.

I wouldn't do that if I were you.

The dagger came down with as much force as Elowen could muster and, for a second, it seemed to connect with it. Then, suddenly, there was a great bang and Elowen was thrown backwards off the chair, hitting the opposite wall with enough force to render her breathless. She landed on her backside, eyes wide, stunned.

She heard footsteps outside. The eye narrowed.

I think not.

The lock in the door turned, snicking into place, just as the handle began to move. The door rattled but stayed shut. A voice called from behind the door in concern.

"Elowen," called Hally. "Are you okay?"

Tell her to go away.

Trying hard not to let her fear leak into her voice, she said as clearly and calmly as possible, "Yes, just fell backwards off my chair."

There was a pause, and then Hally replied, "Why did you lock the door?"

"I'd like to be alone, please, Hally. I'll speak to you tomorrow." She bit her lip, hoping she had been dismissive enough. She almost breathed a sigh of relief as she heard the floorboards creak as Hally moved away.

"What is happening," said Elowen, more to herself, running her fingers through her hair. She had no idea what to do - she felt utterly trapped. "What are you," she asked the voice again, her heart hammering and her hands trembling.

I am an Ornette, though, before, I was something Other.

"Other?"

A creature from the time of the War of Eternal Regret, now trapped in this Ornette.

"Why were you trapped," Elowen asked, though could guess the answer.

For the safety of those around me.

Elowen stood up and moved to the small mirror hanging beside the door to observe the pendant hanging from her neck. She glanced briefly at herself, noting her worried expression and pinched features. Then she looked at the pendant, watching it blink back up at her. The ruby shone stark against her pale skin and the gold twinkled in the light of the room's lamp. The spears jutting out of the top and bottom of the pendant suddenly looked far more dangerous than they had before. She gulped slightly, again trying to take the necklace off, to no avail.

"What do you want with me?" asked Elowen warily, finally giving up. She couldn't believe Imogen had given her such a dangerous object. Had she known there was more to the Ornette than its beauty as a piece of jewellery?

I am here to help you. Gifted to you by your family, I am to be your servant.

"How do I know you won't kill me in my sleep."

I cannot kill, only aid.

"What are you," whispered Elowen again.

I was once like you. I was a Newid with a Wizard father who used me, his only son, to do experimental magic on, much like your grandmother did. Thus, we are the same, but opposites.

"Opposites?"

I chose the path of power. You still have your own path to choose.

"Why are you in the Ornette?" Elowen touched the pendant gingerly, curiously.

The Ornette is a powerful device used for containing souls. I was the only being strong enough to bind those souls.

"Did you just say souls?" Elowen demanded, her stomach dropping with dread.

The souls of the departed Newids.

"Which Newids?!" she almost shouted in shock and dismay. Was she wearing souls around her neck? What did that make her? She had always read that souls should never be used outside of the owner's body, though the Coven of the Dark had experimented with it many times. She blanched as she remembered Imogen's words. She was a Coven of the Dark Enchantress. Did that make her evil, like them?

The eye blinked at her as though surprised. *You mean to say you do not know the prophecy that was made before you were born?* When she did not answer, it continued: *It is a prophecy of old, from the land of Arantaea of Mid-Eberra, told thousands of years ago:*

Once myth and legend become truth,

And the wolves of Raethen howl as one
the aged will inevitably turn to the youth,
To show that a new age has begun.
The sky will burn bright with fire
And the girl with mixed blood
Will call in, with vengeance, a new empire
She who was once taken and lost
Will, by the new moon, thrice be crossed
Arantaea will either flourish in her care
or, under him, crumble into ruin and despair.

"What does that have to do with me?" asked Elowen, confusion pulling at her brows.

It was believed you were the one of whom the prophecy spoke.

"But the prophecy could mean anyone! It did not speak of me specifically." She shook her head as though saying this would make what she said true.

Your grandmother did everything in her power to make sure it was you. You are my equal, the only mimic alive-

"Mimic?" Elowen shook her head. She had heard that word before, used only once in history, from thousands of years ago. The history books spoke of a man, devastatingly beautiful and deadly, who was a 'mimic'. A being of extraordinary power that had been made to fight in the War of Eternal Regret. And as though something clicked, she said, "You are Brannon the Destroyer."

As if having said an incantation to a spell, the Ornette suddenly began to glow blood red and an inky substance began to fall from it onto the floor, leaving the Ornette dull and dim. The substance began to pool and shift, a whirlpool of power, and within seconds, a massive black dog sat before her with glowing red eyes. It bowed its head slightly then began to speak again through her mind.

Thank you, Mistress.

Its voice was cold and dark, barely more than a whisper. The voice sent chills up Elowen's spine and she took a step back, bumping into the wall behind her. In the mirror she was pale, and terror was etched upon her face.

"What... what happened?" whispered Elowen shaking her head as though not quite believing her eyes.

By naming me, you attuned to the Ornette. I can roam freely, but I am still bound to you, to the souls.

"I don't want this," cried Elowen. "I never asked for this." Elowen rubbed her face with her hands, feeling suddenly weak. Stumbling slightly, she collapsed onto the bed beside her gear, breathing heavily. "What's happening to me?" She tried to reach for the second dagger, her only thought to protect herself from this being: Brannon the Destroyer. She knew if history could be believed, that if he had wanted to, he could have killed her in seconds, yet that didn't stop her from needing the comfort of a hilt in her hands. But she was too weak, and the weapons too far.

Attunement takes energy, Brannon explained softly. *You have been weakened by it. You should lie down, Mistress.*

"I am not your Mistress!" Elowen rasped, gasping as she lay down on the mattress, her legs shaking with the effort. "I am Elowen. Elowen Farrowspire." She had never felt so drained, so terrified at how weak she was.

Sleep, mistress. Your energy will be back tomorrow. Attunement is a necessary part-

"I never asked for this," she repeated, desperately wishing she could stop whatever was happening to her.

The dog jumped onto the bed and in a second had transformed, like shimmering liquid, into a small black cat, with the same red eyes, that curled up against Elowen, as though to comfort her. Then she felt a sense of peace rush through her as the cat stared into her eyes.

"What are you doing to me?" Elowen's voice was no more than a whisper.

You can trust me to help you whenever you need me. I am your servant.

"You... you called me a mimic."

The dark cat stared at her with his red eyes and said, *Haven't you ever experienced a time where you were not you but something else entirely? Have you ever experienced a Change before, a shift in your being?*

And like a dream, Elowen could see, as though she were reliving it, a night many years back when she had been wandering the streets of the Lower Section and had come across some men who had wanted to kill her. She remembered wearing a thick black jacket, pants and boots that night to counter the frigid air that had settled upon the Lower Section like an icy blanket. She had been walking home when four men stepped out of a dark alley and surrounded her, their faces pulled into ugly scowls. She recognised them as the leaders of four of the biggest gangs of the Lower Section.

"Your time here is over," she heard one of them say as though she were standing there in front of them again. The same fear and dread that had rushed through her then rushed through her now. What was happening? Where was she?

The men drew closer, their heavy leather cloaks brushing against Elowen as they began jostling her. One of them drew out a knife, and the others grabbed her to hold her firmly. She pulled against them, trying desperately to free herself. Then the one gang leader placed the knife against her throat and pressed it hard against her skin. She felt a warmth trickle down her neck; he had drawn blood.

She tried to scream, adrenalin now pumping through her, but they covered her mouth so that she could barely breathe. She pulled and pushed, and tried to bite down, but to no avail. Fear coursed through her and she felt a shiver run up and down her spine, a shiver that called her to fight and not to give up.

She narrowed her eyes as her silent scream turned into a silent roar. And as though she had unlocked some part of her, she heard words rush through her mind, over and over:

She who mimics will be remade. She who mimics will be remade. She who mimics-

She saw tendrils of darkness extend from her and wrap around her as though lovingly embracing her. The four men took a surprised step back as they watched Elowen disappear behind a purplish-black mist. Seconds passed as the mist swirled around Elowen like a vortex and then, just as soon as it had begun, it stopped and before the men was a great beast, a massive wolf of pure darkness, its dark fur gobbling up the light around it, its purple eyes taking in its prey.

Elowen had felt the shift, could see the paws, feel the fangs. She wanted to tear, wanted to rip and kill, but the savagery was held back by iron-hard logic and reason that reminded her who she was: Elowen Farrowspire.

With one swipe, the men were knocked prone, utterly still and quiet; unconscious. With one last look, Elowen padded away into the night, unaware that she was being watched, unaware that someone would remember.

Elowen was suddenly pulled back into the room above the tavern, as though her mind had left for a second to relive the memory. She felt disoriented and confused, a sort of whiplash effect from being pulled from the memory into the present. It was a memory she had not remembered until now, as though it had been hidden in a deep pocket of her mind. How could she have forgotten something so important?

"What just happened?" she whispered, her eyes wide from shock.

I helped you remember, purred Brannon, his tail flicking lazily.

"So that was real? That really happened?"

Of course, he replied quietly. *You are a Mimic.*

"But what does that mean?" she demanded impatiently.

"You have the ability to shapeshift into any creature you have seen before. You have mimicry magic in your blood from your Enchantress heritage and shapeshifting from your Newid heritage."

"And the Ornette?"

The Ornette helps focus your powers.

Elowen took a deep breath, She felt so weak, so confused. She wanted nothing more than to close her eyes and sleep for the rest of eternity, but she pushed herself onto her elbow and said through gritted teeth, "I can't be a mimic. I can't be the one of whom the prophecy speaks. I don't have magic or shapeshifting powers. The time in the Lower Section was a mistake. I will never be able to do it again." She collapsed back onto the bed as though the effort of saying all that had drained the last of her energy.

Brannon stood and stretched, arching his back. He sat and began cleaning himself, looking so like a normal cat that Elowen thought for a second she was going crazy. Then he looked up at her again with his red eyes, narrowing them slightly as he considered her.

You will experience the Change again. It cannot be avoided - it is who you are. I will help you to realise your full abilities and become the powerful mimic you were meant to be.

"And what if I just want to be Elowen," she whispered bleakly, "And not some mimic? What if I never want to use those powers?"

Then we will all be doomed.

"Why?" she demanded softly.

The War of Fiendish Malice needs a fighter with your powers.

"No."

Brannon cocked his head.

"I will not be some pawn in someone else's war," Elowen snarled.

You will have to face your grandmother sometime.

"No," she repeated, her voice fading and her eyes fluttering as she struggled to keep them open.

Brannon stood and climbed onto Elowen's chest, looking her in the eyes, seriously.

Sleep, Elowen. There is time yet to make those kinds of choices and now is not it. Sleep.

So Elowen closed her eyes, weak and exhausted, and was asleep in seconds, breathing deeply.

Brannon stared at her. *You will fight, my mistress. You will beg to fight.*

And as if her subconscious could hear Brannon, Elowen began to sleep fitfully, dreaming of wars and Shikari and Newids and Enchantresses, all fighting Elowen, who cowered in fear. No Change, no magic, just plain, weak Elowen, dying. And she couldn't fight. Not yet. And so, as if Pamor felt Elowen's terror, it called to her.

Come, Elowen. Let me train you. Let me prepare you. Tomorrow our adventure will begin.

Chapter 9

Pamor Tower

The following day brought with it the promise of adventure. The sky was a bright, periwinkle blue with puffs of clouds sprinkled across it like little white flowers, and the sun shone down upon the land with a welcoming warmth. A mile from the entrance to Illfang city on a narrow dirt road, a small party of a dozen Tournament entrants, dressed in black, rode on horseback toward Pamor Tower. A soft wind rustled through the trees on either side of the road, as though whispering encouragement to the riders. On that wind, a large raven with red eyes could be seen dipping ever so often above the tops of the trees, following close to his mistress.

The excitement was almost palatable and they sat comfortably on their horses in groups of two, chatting about the first day of training. Two riders rode some way behind the others, the one wrestling with her chestnut mare and cursing colourfully under her breath, the other chuckling as she watched from her bay gelding.

Just then, the mare reared, whinying angrily as Elowen grabbed a fistful of its mane in surprise. A few of the other entrants looked back, amused, as Elowen struggled to regain control. Hally, taking pity on her companion, pulled her gelding alongside Elowen's and grabbed the mare's reins, steading the chestnut and calming it with soft 'shushing' sounds.

"This is ridiculous," fumed Elowen when the mare finally took to a steady trot. She tucked the escaped Ornette back behind her shirt.

Hally smiled from her horse and replied, "I can't imagine what you mean."

Elowen glared at Hally. "I most obviously got the worst one. Duchess is all stubbornness and mean-spiritedness." As if to prove her point, Duchess nodded her head, pulling against the reins, and gave a loud 'neigh'.

"She should be perfect for you, then," laughed Hally. "You're both two peas in a pod."

"Come on, Hally," Elowen whined. "Let me ride yours, just for today. Kent is the perfect horse for someone like me."

"A terrible rider, you mean?"

Elowen raised her eyebrow and retorted, "Not all of us are secretly a Shikari spy with years of experience riding horses."

Hally grimaced and said, "I said I'm sorry, Elowen. Are you going to harp on about that for this whole trip?"

Elowen shrugged. "Maybe."

"Then, I think I'll keep this horse. He is mine, after all."

"Fine," Elowen said, digging the heels of her riding boots into Duchess's side to make her hurry up. Duchess, instead, stopped completely, causing Elowen to huff and throw up her hands in frustration.

"OI!" she heard the voice of Buze shout from ahead. "HURRY UP BACK THERE!"

Duchess, as if understanding this, suddenly lurched forward into a quick trot, and Elowen, whose hands had still been raised, had to grab the pommel of the saddle. Hally clapped her hand to her mouth to stop from giggling.

"Perhaps you're right," grinned Hally as Kent matched Duchess's trot. "She does seem to have a mind of her own."

"Who, the rider, or the horse?" a smooth, male voice said.

Hally and Elowen looked up to find that the two entrants ahead of them had slowed to a stop, waiting for Hally and Elowen to catch up.

The one who had spoken was handsome with dark hair and eyes, full lips that were curved in a half-smile, and broad shoulders that pulled at the black jacket he wore. The other rider was a girl with long blonde hair and blue eyes, her lips pulled in a thin line of annoyance. She was the only other girl who had a similar build to Elowen.

Hally snorted, replying, "The rider, of course."

The girl rolled her eyes and said, "Come on, Damien. Let's go."

Damien did not answer immediately, instead considering Elowen thoughtfully with that same half smile that sent butterflies fluttering through Elowen's stomach, before saying, "You go ahead, Madelyn. We can talk later."

Madelyn narrowed her eyes before yanking her horse around, and nudging it into a trot, leaving Elowen, Hally and Damien to follow slowly in her wake. Damien chuckled once Madelyn had ridden some way out of earshot.

"You'll have to forgive Madelyn," he said quietly, positioning his horse beside Hally's (much to Elowen's disappointment). "She is not used to sharing."

"You seem to take pleasure in aggravating her," remarked Elowen, raising her eyebrow at him.

Damien grinned and replied, "You figured me out. So, may I ask what I may call you lovely ladies?"

Hally exchanged a glance with Elowen, before saying, "I'm Hally, Hally Marsin, and this is Elowen Farrowspire."

"A pleasure to meet you both," said Damien smoothly, bowing his head slightly. "I'm Damien Drovenshere. Is this your first time entering the tournament?"

Elowen nodded and Damien smiled warmly. "Best of luck, then. This is my second time."

"I wasn't aware that you could try multiple times," said Elowen, surprised.

Hally answered, "If you show potential, they allow it. I, too, entered twice. The first time I failed one challenge, but managed to pass every other one quite well."

"Quite well?" snorted Damien. "Don't be so modest. I remember the year you entered. You were brilliant but unlucky."

Hally smiled. "Thanks."

Elowen frowned. "Are there many entrants who are here for a second time?"

"Half of the group is doing this again," replied Damien. "The other half, like you, is new."

"That seems unfair. How am I to compete with them."

Hally shook her head. "El, there's no competition. They would allow all the entrants into the Shikari if you all passed. You just need to focus on yourself."

"I would recommend befriending a returning entrant, though," said Damien. "You can learn a lot from them."

Elowen laughed and said, "What, such as yourself?"

Damien grinned. "I accept."

"Why?" asked Hally, confused. "You don't even know us."

He shrugged. "Let's just say I have a knack for being a good judge of character."

Hally snorted in a most unladylike way and replied, "And what a happy coincidence that your father is Master Gimrad."

Elowen was stunned. "You must know a lot about all of us already."

Damien smiled and shrugged. "Perhaps that would mean something if I were one of my five older brothers, but my father doesn't have much time for me. So no, I don't know much. What I do know, however, is that you," he looked at Elowen curiously, "were spoken for by my father when you were failed by that idiot Buze. Now, why would that be, I wonder." He raised his eyebrow questioningly.

"No idea," answered Elowen with a sigh. It was a question that had been plaguing her since she had heard this news. She glanced at

Damien and found him watching her intently, a strange look on his face. She blushed and looked away quickly. She couldn't fathom why someone so handsome would rather ride with them than with someone like Madelyn, who was just as gorgeous as he was.

A surprisingly comfortable silence followed. Up ahead, the other riders were pulling off to the side of the road where a pretty green area under some thick trees beckoned them to rest. Elowen, Hally and Damien pulled their horses to the side and dismounted, tying the reins to a nearby tree. Brannon landed on a high branch in the tree, bowing his head slightly when Elowen looked up and met his red eyes.

In her mind, she heard him speak: *Nothing to report, Mistress. All is safe.*

Elowen gave a curt nod, as surreptitiously as she could; she wasn't sure if she was ready to share Brannon's existence with Hally, or anyone else. Then they took a seat close to the other entrants, who had all seemed to form their own groups of three or four entrants. Buze stood in front of the group, his face pulled in his usual expression of discontent, speaking quietly to two other Shikari who had ridden with the party.

Finally, he turned to the group and said loudly, "Right, you lot. We will stop here for no longer than thirty minutes to eat and rest. I hope you all remembered to bring a ration pack." His expression suggested he did not care whether they had, or had not. He turned and went to his horse, a beautiful black stallion who had just as mean a temperament as its rider, and began rummaging in his pack. The entrants looked at each other quickly before doing the same. Once they had all sat down again, Buze choosing a spot with the other Shikari as far from the entrants as possible, they all began munching on apples and dried meat.

Damien took a bite out of his apple before turning to Elowen and Hally. "Do you both feel ready for the tournament?"

Elowen's stomach did a wild flip and she bit her lip nervously as she thought of the tournament. She answered truthfully, "I don't feel ready, and I can't even believe I'm actually going to do this tournament." She ran her fingers through her hair before tugging worriedly on her ponytail. "What was I thinking?" she said quietly.

Damien nodded and Hally looked sympathetically at Elowen. Damien eventually said, "I felt the same way last year, but the training leading up to the tournament really makes a difference. You'll be more than ready by the time the tournament arrives. Don't stress."

Elowen nodded but didn't feel much more confident at his words. What if she was the worst entrant? What if she embarrassed herself? Hally reached over and squeezed her hand comfortingly.

"At least you won't be alone, El," she said encouragingly.

"Speaking of, where is your partner?" Elowen asked Damien curiously.

"At Pamor Tower," he replied, taking a swig from his waterskin.

"What's Pamor Tower like," asked Elowen, reaching for the waterskin that she had placed next to her leg.

Hally smiled and said, "It's amazing. One of the wonders of Arantaea. It's a massive stone tower that reaches high above the mountains surrounding it. Each level is a different area, with the top levels being the sleeping quarters of the Shikari and the lower levels being for the entrants and, after the Tournament, the new Shikari. The ground floor is the stables with the floor above being the kitchen, followed by the mess hall. Some of the other levels include the different training areas for entrants and Shikari."

"Why don't you live there," asked Damien, ripping his dried meat in half with his teeth.

"She was too busy spying on me," replied Elowen, pursing her lips.

Hally rolled her eyes and said, "I was too busy making a best friend out of you, whether you believe me or not. You know, I stopped reporting back to Shikari after we became friends."

"Friends don't lie."

Hally sighed. "Grow up, El. The world isn't so black and white."

Elowen looked away, blushing slightly. She knew she was being childish, so she nodded and said, "Fine, but from now on, no lies."

Hally smiled warmly, a look of relief passing across her face. "We'll make a good team for this tournament, El. I won't let you lose."

The sun had reached its highest point in the sky by the time they finished and mounted their horses again. Damien remained with them for the remainder of the trip, telling them all he knew about the other entrants.

"The two boys in the front are called Gerard and Hant. Both are returning for their second time, though they are not the nicest entrants, so perhaps don't try to befriend them." Elowen had to agree that they did not look to be at all friendly. Both had tanned faces and were well-built, but while Gerard had no hair, Hant had long hair tied at the nape of his neck.

"Behind them are Jessaly and Kimiad. Jessaly is quite a sweet girl who is also here for the second year, and Kimiad is her brother, who is here for the first time this year. Then, you know Madelyn. This is her first time, as it is Clarissa and Pollok's, the girl and boy riding on either side of her." Jessaly and Kimiad both had dark skin and hair, while Clarissa had light brown hair and Pollok had black hair and narrow eyes. The five of them were riding close together and chatting loudly about the tournament and comparing how prepared they each were.

"In front of us are Dros and Mol. This is their second time, too." Both Dros and Mol were large and fit, with short black hair and pale skin. They glanced back at the sound of their names and Damien raised his hand in greeting. They nodded their heads and turned back to the front. "They look intimidating, but I respect them both and recommend befriending them during our training."

Elowen nodded, repeating the names of the other entrants in an effort to remember them - she was normally terrible at remembering names. All the entrants looked fit and ready for the tournament, which made Elowen more nervous. She already felt like an outsider next to all these rich boys and girls, though at least, according to Damien, they were all around Elowen's age, with only one or two years difference between them.

The rest of the ride was uneventful, and by the time the sun had begun to set, Elowen's thighs and buttocks were feeling considerably achy. They had begun a slow trek up and around the side of a tall mountain that was surrounded by other mountains. The horses moved in single file now and Elowen nervously looked over the side of the trail, down the steep mountain, to the bottom where many rocks were piled.

"How much longer?" she groaned, shifting in her saddle.

"We should see the tower soon," replied Hally.

She was right. After a few minutes, the horses rounded the mountain and ahead of them rose the magnificent tower. It was an impressive sight, its gargantuan size towering over the mountains surrounding it. The entrants seeing the tower for the first time were all gobsmacked, staring at the tower with their mouths open and their eyes wide.

"Welcome to Pamor," said Damien from behind her. "Impressive, no?"

Elowen nodded, then groaned when she saw how much road stood between them and the bridge leading to the middle of the tower. They continued their trek for another hour until the sun had fully set and night spread across the sky with millions of stars scattered across it. Lights from the many windows around the tower shone out welcomingly, beckoning the entrants with the promise of rest. Brannon soared overhead toward the tower, circling it once before landing on one of the upper levels.

As they drew closer to the tower, the road opened up, leading away from the mountain and to a wide stone bridge. Horse hooves clip-clopped over the bridge as the tower loomed ahead of them and, at the opposite end of the bridge, large wooden doors opened into a bright entrance hall. As they passed through the front doors, two Shikari guards in black Shikari uniforms on either side of the doors bowed to Buze and waved cheerfully at the entrants.

The Entrance hall was massive, with pairs of brass candelabra wall lamp sconces lining the wall of the tower and glass windows reflecting the light. A group of servants dressed in white uniforms of a similar style to the Shikari's uniform stood waiting for them.

Buze, the other Shikari and the entrants all dismounted, the servants rushing forward to lead the horses away to the stables. Once they had all disappeared, Buze spoke, his voice echoing across the entrance hall.

"We will now make our way down to the mess hall to have dinner, after which you will be taken to your dormitory to rest. Follow me.

Across the hall was another set of doors opening up to a wide stairwell that ran along the side of the tower. Its lack of a railing made Elowen feel slightly sick at the thought of having to go up and down those stairs. When they began to descend the stairs, Elowen noticed a warmth that did not fit the outside of the tower; she had assumed it would be windy and cold with the mountains and their snowy tops surrounding the tower. She paused on the way down and curiously reached her hand out to the edge of the stairwell. Her hand met a barrier that was naked to the eye. She pulled her hand back, surprised.

"Magic," she whispered to herself. Damien walked up beside her and leaned against the barrier, though not seeming to be leaning against anything at all. Elowen had to stop herself from grabbing him. He grinned as though aware she would have attempted to save him.

"A masterpiece of human, dwarf and Enchantress work," he said before continuing down the stairs with Elowen and Hally following close behind.

"The dwarves and Enchantresses helped?" said Elowen, surprised. She had not been aware that the two races had any kind of relationship with the humans; the dwarves were renowned for their mastery in construction, though they usually never interacted with other races, while the Enchantresses also tended to keep themselves and their magic away from the humans.

Darwin nodded, though somewhat sadly. "It was long ago, around the year 4723 DB, when the dwarves were slaves and the Wives of Ember had an agreement with the Shikari. Now, the dwarves keep to themselves and the Wives of Ember only occasionally help us with our magical needs."

They reached the lower part of the tower just as Elowen's legs began to feel like they would crumble beneath her, and they all followed Buze into the mess hall. It was slightly larger than the Entrance Hall; Pamor Tower was larger at the bottom, with the battlements at the top being the smallest part. The mess hall walls were also lined with brass candelabra, and several large, circular tables were arranged in a semicircle around a large stage in the middle of the room. The table at the far end was the only rectangular table in the room with chairs seated along one side facing the other tables and stage. Other Shikari already sat at different tables, with the table at the far end that only had chairs on the outside seating the Shikari leaders that Elowen had met previously. Master Gimrad's chair was empty, as was the chair beside it. In the centre of the room was a large stage where musicians sat playing instruments - lutes, violas, flutes and drums - and filling the room with a merry tune. Buze made his way to the second empty seat and sat down, immediately reaching toward the buffet of food that was spread across the Masters' table, as were the other tables for the rest of the Shikari.

Elowen's tummy grumbled hungrily as the entrants made their way to the empty seats at the outer edge of the table closest to the door. The feast looked so inviting that some of the entrants immediately began piling food onto their silver plates. There was such a wide selection of meats and vegetables, soups and pies, and desserts, that Elowen couldn't keep her mouth from hanging open in shock; this was more food than she had eaten in a week.

As she sat down between Hally and Damien and began reaching for the roast chicken pieces, roast potatoes and peas, the door to the hall opened again and in walked a middle-aged man with long dark hair tied at the nape of his neck. He, too, wore the black Shikari uniform with the metal emblem pinned to his front, though his emblem was gold rather than silver.

He strode purposefully to the centre of the room where the platform stood. The musicians immediately stopped playing and looked expectantly at this man, as did the rest of the Shikari. A hush fell over the hall.

He smiled warmly and said, "Welcome, all, to Pamor Tower."

Chapter 10

Settling in

"**I** am Lord Kimrad, and it gives me great pleasure to welcome you to the home of the Shikari." Lord Kimrad opened his arms wide in a gesture of welcome. His face was warm as he smiled round at them, but his eyes remained cool and calculating. Elowen wondered what those eyes had seen in his time as a Shikari.

He continued, "You have travelled long and far, so I will not bore you with too long a speech. I only wish to say that I hope you will eat and be merry, for tomorrow your training starts, and it will not be easy. The coming days will see you participate in a series of tests that will determine your abilities. At the end of the tests, you will be placed in a group of similar abilities and skills and you will use the rest of the time to train hard before the start of the Tournament. Please be sure to make use of all equipment and trainers at your disposal. Should you, at any point, wish to back out of the tournament, we will not stop you. I need not remind you that this tournament has seen many injuries, some deadly, and though we will do our best to ensure your safety, we cannot make any promises. You must, therefore, be absolutely certain before taking part in the tournament." Silence followed his words with a few entrants shifting in their seats as though eager to prove themselves. Elowen tugged nervously on her ponytail as her stomach did a weird flip-flop.

Lord Kimrad continued after a short pause, "Alright, then, dig in, everybody." He gave them one last smile before making his way to the large, throne-like seat at the centre of the main table. He sat and reached for his silver goblet before leaning toward Buze and striking up a conversation with him. A pleasant hum filled the hall again as everyone began talking. The music swelled as the musicians began playing a merry jig that had Elowen tapping her foot with the tune. She took a bite of her roast potatoes, savouring the flavours that danced on her tongue, as, opposite her, Dros and Mol began speaking to Damien about the previous year's Tournament in between mouthfuls of butternut soup.

"Remember that one boy who lost his eye?" Drol was saying, his voice higher than Elowen had expected. He had a pleasant, but serious face that made him look older than she suspected he was.

"Yeah, and we called him 'Morkos,'" laughed Mol, a deep, throaty laugh. He, too, looked serious, though he had a twinkle in his eyes that made Elowen instantly like him.

Elowen frowned at the unfamiliarity of the word. "Morkos?" she repeated, thinking hard to remember if she had heard it before.

"Af'r un-geyed weeta ee-a naima," said Hally, her mouth full of bread. She swallowed with effort, then tried again, "After the one-eyed creature that feeds on nightmares."

"Will we have to fight that in the Labyrinth?" asked Elowen, concerned, causing her voice to rise slightly in pitch. She coughed embarrassedly.

Damien shrugged nonchalantly. "The Labyrinth changes every year so you never know what you're going to get." He ripped a large piece of turkey off with his teeth.

Elowen raised her eyebrow, confused. "So they build a new labyrinth each year?" She tried to imagine what the Labyrinth would look like - would it be made with stone or hedges of plants or perhaps wood?

Dros and Mol exchanged a glance. "The Labyrinth is the Labyrinth," said Dros slowly, as though not certain of Elowen's question.

Hally rolled her eyes. "That clears that up." She turned to Elowen and asked. "Did Imogen not tell you about the Labyrinth?"

Elowen shook her head, beginning to wish she hadn't said anything. It seemed she still had a lot to learn in comparison with the others. They all exchanged a glance again, before Damien said, "Well, no one knows for sure, but it is believed that the Labyrinth is 'alive'. The doors never lead to the same places because the 'keys' to open the doors change. Then again, it could also be because of the boatmen.... You know, the Transporters who take us across the Tenebris." When Elowen continued to look unsure, Damien's eyebrows disappeared behind his fringe in concern. "You might want to spend some time in the library to get familiar with Marasae. Anyway, the Transporters take us all across the river from the main entrance to the second, and, because there are so many entrances, you never know what you will get. That's why it's so important to follow your map once you're inside."

Elowen's stomach dropped. "I have to read a map?" When they nodded, she cursed under her breath. She had never been very good at reading, and she had never needed a map before, so the chances of her getting lost were high. Hally seemed to understand because she reached over and squeezed her hand consolingly.

"I'll be with you all the way," she whispered so that only Elowen could hear. "It's easy to get lost, but there are ways to find your way back with the Locator. The leaders wouldn't let you get stuck in the labyrinth."

Elowen nodded, feeling slightly relieved, though still nervous. She tried to focus on what the others were saying.

"So, who will your partner be this year?" Dros was asking Damien while helping himself to a massive piece of lamb. Damien looked uncomfortable and she saw him glance at the main table before saying, "My, uh, father."

Mol choked on his goblet of mulled wine, spluttering as he turned to Damien and coughed out, "Your father? What happened to the partner you had last year?"

Damien looked even more uncomfortable as he answered, "My father sent Jolion to the Bastion of the Shadow Count. He seemed to think she was to blame for me not getting through the tournament."

They all looked nervously up at Gimrad before Hally said, "I've heard that the Buzirukth Crags where it is located are home to some really terrifying creatures." She shuddered. "I would not go there if my life depended on it."

Elowen reached for a slice of white cake and said to Dros and Mol, "So who are your partners?"

Dros nodded his head to the table to the right of the main table. "See that man with the goatee and bald head? That's Yollic, my partner. And the man next to him with the golden hair is Harold, Mol's partner."

They spent the next half an hour getting to know each other and finishing their food. As the evening crept on and Elowen's trousers were feeling considerably tighter, she began to feel drowsy and comfortably full for the first time in a long time. She helped herself to one last piece of white cake, which had quickly become her favourite dessert.

Mol put down his silver spoon and rubbed his belly in content. "That's me," he started, belching slightly. "I'm going to head to the dormitory."

He was not the only one who stood; several other Shikari and entrants began pushing their chairs back and standing. Elowen looked around quickly, putting her silver fork down beside her half-finished cake. Hally, wiping her mouth with a napkin, also stood and stretched. Then she turned to Elowen and said, "I'm going to head to my rooms."

Elowen pushed back her chair, wincing as it made a loud scraping sound as it slid across the stone floor. She nodded and received a tight hug from Hally.

"Get some rest - you'll need it for tomorrow," she muttered into Elowen's ear. Then Hally made her way across the hall to the doors leading to the staircase. She disappeared out the door, followed by several other Shikari.

"Shall we head up?" asked Damien from beside her. Elowen nodded and began following the crowd heading out the door.

The staircase outside took them up several levels before they finally reached the door to the dormitory. Elowen clutched a stitch at her side as they made their way into the dormitory.

It was a large, circular room with lush, red carpets spread across the floor. There were fifteen single dark blue beds lining the wall, each situated between tall windows set in alcoves with long window benches at the bottom. Drawers were set into the benches where other entrants were already transferring their clothes from the bags that had been brought up for them. Beside each bed was a wooden screen to dress behind. In the centre of the room was a lounge with brown leather couches and comfortable-looking, red armchairs. Lanterns with magicked lights hung from the ceiling beside each bed providing a soft, warm glow. At the far end were open double doors that led into a bathroom.

Damien made his way to a bed, then glanced back at Elowen who was still basking in the welcoming atmosphere of the room. Giving a small wave, he said a quick goodnight to her, then began unpacking his bag. Elowen's eyes roved over the beds in search of her tattered bag. She spotted it on the opposite side of the dormitory to Damien's bed. It appeared the boys had one-half of the dormitory while the girls occupied the other half.

Elowen made her way to her bed in the middle of the girl's side of the dormitory. There was a window beside her bed through which she almost instantly noted Brannon perched outside it. She opened the window with a small crack and instantly a black moth flew in and landed on her bed, transforming into a black cat and closing his eyes, pretending to sleep. Elowen smiled slightly; she was becoming used to having her strange friend of a sort with her, giving her peace of mind.

To the left of her bed, Madelyn was already unpacking her things while chatting enthusiastically with Clarissa, who was lying on the bed beside the door. Jessaly stood behind the wooden screen to the right of Elowen's bed, beginning to dress herself in her nightclothes, and she smiled as Elowen sat on her bed. Elowen smiled back tentatively.

"You're Elowen, right?" asked Jessaly as she pulled socks over her feet. She had a soft, pleasant voice that didn't quite match her stature.

Elowen nodded and Jessaly smiled, sitting down on her bed facing Elowen. "I'm Jess." Then, suddenly noticing Brannon, she said, "Oh, how cute! Is that your familiar?"

Elowen smiled. "Yes, I suppose he is. This is Brannon."

Brannon purred softly in response, earning a stroke of the head from Elowen. He opened his eyes to look at Jessaly, who jumped back slightly.

"Oh, my, he has rather strange eyes." She shook her head and looked away, somewhat disturbed. "So how are you feeling about training tomorrow?"

"Honestly, quite nervous."

Jess nodded understandingly. "I was nervous, too, last year. This time, I feel a bit more ready, you know. Do you know what you'll focus on in training tomorrow?" When Elowen shook her head, Jess continued, "I think I might focus on survival tactics. That was the one thing I did really badly last year."

Elowen bit her lip nervously. What would she focus on tomorrow? Truth be told, she had no idea if her training over the last few years had paid off.

"What are you good at?" asked Jess curiously.

"What do you mean?"

"Well, you must be good at something if you were nominated to enter the Tournament."

Elowen grew quiet as she thought back on the last few years she had spent preparing for the tournament. She knew the skills that she hadn't needed a partner to practice would be good, but the other skills she had tried to focus on had never developed, mostly because she had always practised them alone when she needed a partner. And so, she answered, hesitantly, "I am quite good with a bow and arrow and knife throwing."

She heard a snicker behind her and turned to find Madelyn exchanging a look with Clarissa. Both girls grinned nastily.

"I suppose you think you have a chance of getting through the tournament with those skills," said Madelyn, smirking.

Elowen frowned as Jess said, "What's your problem?"

Madelyn shrugged and replied, "I just don't think we should be encouraging Lowers to enter the tournament."

"She was chosen, as you were," Jess said, "so I don't see what the problem is."

"Yes, by a failed Shikari," snapped Madelyn. She looked at Elowen and narrowed her eyes. "You don't belong here. Go home."

Elowen stared at Madelyn, heat pouring into her face. She felt her eyes drifting past Madelyn and Clarissa as she realised the room had suddenly gone quiet. She noticed Damien staring at the two of them, his hand paused over his bag. Gerard and Hant lazed on the one sofa, and both narrowed their eyes at Elowen as she looked at them. Kimiad lay on his bed playing with a knife and though he wasn't looking their way, he had an uncomfortable look on his face. In the corner of the room, Dros, Mol and Pollok stood looking on curiously, both Dros and Mol frowning at Madelyn.

She turned back to find Madelyn suddenly standing a lot closer. Elowen stood quickly and Madelyn grabbed her arm tightly.

"Go home, rat," she whispered into Elowen's ear.

"Or what?" Elowen wrenched her arm free and glared at Madelyn. She hated that word and she felt her temper rising.

"Or I'll make sure you regret it." Madelyn stepped back and turned her back to Elowen, then said loudly, "You stink, rat. I don't want you sleeping next to my bed. Move."

Elowen rolled her eyes. "I think I'll stay, thanks. You can move if you want." Then she turned her back on Madelyn and began unpacking her bag. She heard Madelyn huff behind her.

Elowen clenched her fist. She was tempted to punch Madelyn, and a strange rage filled her as the word 'rat' went through her head over and over. Then something strange happened: it started with a shiver, quite out of place in this warm and cosy room, and was followed by a roaring in her ears. She felt shaky and queasy all of a sudden and, with the thought of throwing up all over Madelyn spurring her feet to move, she quickly made her way to the bathroom. She could hear laughter behind her but she didn't care. What was happening? She thought as she closed the double doors and leaned against them, breathing deeply.

The bathroom was smaller than the dormitory with wooden cubicles running along the one side and a big bath sunken into the ground in the middle. Sinks lined the other side with mirrors lining the walls above.

She stumbled over to the sink and turned on the water, letting the coolness run through her fingers. She looked up into the gold-bordered mirror in front of her and found herself staring back with wide eyes. She looked pale, almost as pale as her silver hair, and the dark marks that usually stained the underside of her eyes seemed darker. She looked peaky, but she looked... normal. Not how she felt, which was a strange out-of-body feeling.

The pain wracked through her and she doubled over, biting her lip to keep from crying out. She tasted blood and, looking up, she almost fainted at the sight that met her.

Her face was screwed up in pain, and her eyes... her eyes were no longer purple. They were dark brown. She lifted her hand to her face and jumped back as she saw claws protruding from her fingers. The pain continued to pull at her muscles and bones but just as quickly as it had started, the pain stopped. She closed her eyes and took a deep breath. When she opened them again, everything was back to normal. Had she just imagined what she had seen?

The sensation passed, and she was left with a feeling of familiarity, as though she knew the pain. She shook her head slightly in confusion, left the bathroom and changed quickly into her nightwear behind her screen. Then she hopped into bed, where Brannon was curled up in cat form, still considering Madeline darkly. He glanced at her and narrowed his eyes. She heard a voice in her head say:

What happened, Mistress?

Elowen shook her head. Now wasn't the time to talk about what she had just experienced, so she closed her eyes.

It felt like seconds had passed when she suddenly opened her eyes. All was dark and she could hear someone snoring across the room. She must have fallen asleep quite quickly, but something had woken her. She peered around, blinking to get used to the low light levels. A shadow at the end of her bed made her sit up suddenly, her heart thumping hard against her chest. The same shiver ran down her back and she had the same, strange, yet familiar, urge to give in to the sharp and sudden pain she felt. Then it was gone and she heard Damien's voice whispering her name.

"What?" she asked, confused. Her heart was still pumping wildly, but a part of her held its breath in anticipation.

Damien was silent for a second, smiling a small crooked smile that had her heart doing somersaults, then said quietly to Elowen, "I'm going to the rooftop garden. Would you like to come?"

"Okay," replied Elowen, now completely awake. She blushed as her thoughts rushed to what he could want with her there; perhaps this was a date. She hopped out of bed, put on her jacket and followed Damien out of the dormitory.

Just as she passed through the doors, she heard the voice of Brannon say in her head, *Must I come, Mistress?*

Elowen pretended she had not heard and continued down the corridor. She saw the dark form of Brannon follow some distance behind.

The air was cool and a slight wind pulled at Elowen's clothes when they reached the top of the Pamor, after a long and arduous climb around the side of the tower, past the several levels of rooms and, just before reaching the garden, the library. She took a deep breath and felt it catch as she took in the rooftop garden.

It was beautiful, the tranquillity so inviting she felt herself moving forward further into the garden. There were rose bushes and hedges, arches and fountains, purple hydrangeas and soft May bushes, all spaced evenly around swinging benches. In the middle was a white wooden pergola where a circle of comfy benches surrounded a low table that had several books on it. There looked to be a pulley lift that disappeared into the floor below where the library could be found. She felt herself moving toward the pergola, half aware of Damien following slowly behind her, and she sat on the first cushioned bench. She saw Brannon take flight and begin to circle high above them. Suddenly she heard him shout in her head:

Mistress-

"Thank you, Damien," said a voice softly behind her. Jumping up, she whirled around to find Gimrad standing half-hidden in the shadow of the hedge behind the pergola. For the third time, the shiver ran through her and she felt herself baring her teeth in fright, though, at the back of her mind, she wondered at her reaction. A black shape dived out of the sky to land on her shoulder and gave a caw of fury.

Gimrad gave her a smile, which widened as he took in Brannon, and then said, "Miss Farrowspire, a pleasure to finally meet you."

Chapter 11

First Day of Training

"**L**ord Gimrad was there?"

Hally's shocked voice echoed through the large clearing and she received a smart smack on the arm from Elowen.

"Shh," Elowen hissed, glancing around at the other entrants, who luckily seemed too busy concentrating on sparring to notice.

They sat in the centre of a large forest some way up the second largest mountain beside Pamor. It was late afternoon and the sun was slowly descending below the tree line. Elowen had woken early that morning to find the rest of the dormitory already empty and she had hurriedly dressed in a brown tunic and pants and made her way to breakfast, eager to find Hally and share the events of the night before. They had spent the morning on an arduous hike through the forest to this clearing, where a long and difficult obstacle course had been set up for them, disappearing into the trees, along with a sparring field, survival tactics practice area and a make-shift maze that was surprisingly quite large. Elowen and Hally had spent the afternoon practising survival techniques, building fires and shelters, while the rest of the entrants all focused on fighting techniques - Elowen and Hally had wanted to save their strength for the obstacle course challenge that would take place later.

Hally looked around quickly from where they sat, cross-legged, on the dusty ground, pausing her attempt at making a health potion, and said more quietly, "And Damien was the one who brought you to him?"

"Yes, though he didn't tell me beforehand." Elowen glanced at Damien who was sparring with both Dros and Mol, wearing the same brown tunic and pants that all the entrants wore. As if aware of her attention, he paused and glanced at her, receiving a whack from Mol's wooden pole. Rubbing his shoulder, he turned back to the other two and said something, before making his way over to Hally and Elowen. He leaned against his pole and smiled tentatively at Elowen. She glared back at him and Hally huffed quietly.

Grimacing, Damien dropped to a crouch, and said, "I'm really sorry for not warning you before. My father was concerned about your safety as well as keeping your meeting with him a secret from the rest of the entrants." He glanced back in Madelyn's direction. "You can understand that, surely? I meant no harm."

Elowen sighed and looked away. She was tired of being kept in the dark about things, but what he said made sense. Besides that, she also hoped he would never find out how disappointed she had been that their trip to the garden had not, in fact, been a date.

"What did he want, anyway?" Damien continued, lowering his voice further.

Elowen considered not telling him - if his father hadn't deigned to tell him, why should she - but then she noticed Hally looking at her intently, waiting for her answer, so she said, "He had advice... and a warning."

Hally's eyes widened and Damien frowned. Elowen continued, "He advised me to use the resources at Pamor, including letting him help me, and also to trust you," she nodded at Hally, "to do the rest."

Hally nodded slowly, then said, "And the warning?"

Elowen took a breath, stalling as she picked up some random herbs to drop into the concoction they were brewing. Hally put her hand out to stop her, picked up some other herbs and put those in instead.

"What was the warning?" Damien pressed.

Sighing, she said, "There is a danger of which I need to be aware."

Hally shook her head. "But this is the safest place for you. What danger could possibly get past the Shikari?" She picked up their cutting knife and looked around as though expecting someone to jump out of the tree line and attack them.

Damien's knuckles whitened around the wooden pole and he narrowed his eyes, saying, "What danger?"

Elowen took another breath. "Gundrel is here," she said, slowly.

Damien looked confused and Hally said, "Why is that a danger?"

Elowen uncrossed her legs, which had started to get pins and needles, and stretched them out, rubbing the feeling back into them. Noticing movement above her, she glanced up to see Brannon land in a nearby tree.

Crossing her legs again, she began, "Apparently Gundrel wants to kidnap me."

"Wait, wait, wait," said Damien, holding up his hand. "Who is Gundrel?"

"A Newid who helped get Elowen away from the Coven of the Dark," explained Hally, earning an annoyed glance from Elowen - did they really want Damien to know everything? She still hadn't decided whether to trust him or not.

Damien seemed to notice the look Elowen gave Hally and smiled sheepishly. "I know you don't think you can, but trust me. I won't tell anyone." Elowen pursed her lips disbelievingly as he continued, "I heard about that mission. I didn't realise you were the child they had saved. So why, if he had helped you before, is this Newid trying to kidnap you."

Elowen sighed and said, "Your father was very vague when I asked him the same question, but he did let on that they think the Newids want me for the war."

Damien nodded and said, almost to himself, "I got the impression that's why the Shikari want you, too." His eyes widened as though he realised he'd said too much.

Elowen smirked slightly and said, "I know you don't think you can, but trust me. I won't tell anyone."

Damien laughed, a warm sound that had a smile pulling at Elowen's lips. "Touché," he said, still chuckling. "So what makes you so special, Miss Farrowspire?" His eyes twinkled and Elowen's heart stuttered.

Blushing slightly, she said, "I think they are mistaken. There's nothing special about me."

Hally snorted and rolled her eyes. "Come on, El. You can't really believe that. You're half-Newid, half-Enchantress, the first of your kind."

Elowen frowned. "I can't really be the first," she said, remembering what Brannon had said. She considered telling them about Brannon, but something had her hesitating.

"Why not? Enchantresses and Newids have never been on friendly terms. It is taboo to mix bloodlines. Your father and mother would have known that."

"So then why am I here?" Elowen muttered, more to herself than Damien and Hally.

Hally laughed, not unkindly, and patted Elowen on the shoulder. "Love? I don't know. But I think we can say you are special."

Elowen shook her head, stubbornly. "I have never shown magic potential, or shifting abilities," she lied, her mind flying back to the memory of her first Change. She didn't think now was the time to bring that up - it would require more time than she had.

Hally shrugged and began stirring the health potion. "Perhaps you haven't come of age yet. Anyway, why would the Shikari and the Newids and the Enchantresses be trying to get you on their side? They must know you are special. Don't worry, I'm sure we'll find out soon enough. I'd also like to know what he meant by offering you help. The Elder Shikari are technically not meant to help, but I suppose he is the leader, so perhaps the rules don't apply to him."

Elowen paused as she thought. "He said something about the Labyrinth, that its paths do have a logic to them, but I'll need to figure that out for myself. He said something about the library."

Damien nodded. "He said the same thing to me, but I wasn't able to figure it out. The library is huge. I'm not even sure where to start looking for that kind of information. How are we supposed to find anything on it in time?

A loud shout interrupted their musing.

"You three!"

Aavos was standing across the clearing surrounded by the other entrants. They were all looking at the three of them curiously. Aavos held up his hands questioningly. "Are you coming or not?"

Elowen swore under her breath. "Oh no," she muttered as they stood up, quickly bottling the now-ready healing potion, and began making their way across the clearing.

"What?" said Damien and Hally in unison.

"We need to do the obstacle course now," Elowen said back, as though this was obvious.

"Right," said Aavos loudly as Elowen, Damien and Hally joined the crowd of entrants gathered around Aavos. "Now that you're all gathered, it's time to put your endurance to the test. In front of you is the obstacle course you will be doing. It is a long one, split into different sections so that one side is easier and one side is harder. You will be faced with riddles like the ones you will face in the Labyrinth. Should you get them right, you will get the easier course. Get them wrong and you get the harder course. Partners will go with you and try to help." He looked round at them all and grinned. "Good luck to you all. You will need it if you don't have the brains for this." He chuckled nastily then said, "Get into line. I will blow the whistle for each of you, one after the other."

There was a mad scramble as everyone tried to be at the back of the queue. By the time Elowen looked again, she was in the front and

Hally some way toward the back, aghast that Elowen had been so slow. Damien chuckled quietly from behind Elowen as Hally disgruntledly made her way to the front.

"Sorry," whispered Elowen to Hally as the whistle blew.

"Let's go," said Hally, still slightly annoyed, and she grabbed Elowen's hand, pulling her toward the first obstacle: hurdles.

Hally gave Elowen a leg up as they climbed atop the first hurdle and balanced on it. Elowen took a breath and jumped across the gap, wobbling slightly as she landed. Hally scrambled up the side of the first one till she was balanced on top and also jumped across to the second hurdle. Six more hurdles they jumped across, Elowen's calves already beginning to burn with the effort of balancing, but she managed to stay on top.

Walls followed the hurdles, some at an angle with ropes to pull yourself up, and some vertical with holes to climb. They climbed over all four and landed on the other side, Elowen's knees buckling slightly at the impact of the drop. The walls were followed by a water jump and balancing ropes and by the time they had managed to get across, they heard the whistle blow for Damien, who was alone, his father having not arrived for the training.

They reached a tall wooden wall with two doors facing diagonally outward, with the wall then continuing past so that the rest of the obstacle course was hidden. In front of the wall was a man dressed in a Shikari uniform. He took them in as they stopped, panting slightly after the previous obstacles.

"I fly when I'm born, lie down when I'm alive, and run when I'm dead. What am I?" he said quietly so that Elowen had to strain her ears to hear over the sound of the third whistle-blow.

Still panting slightly, Elowen thought long and hard though no answers came to her. She looked at Hally worriedly and noticed Hally smiling.

"Don't worry," she said to Elowen quietly, "I've heard this one before." She turned to the man and said, "A snowflake."

He stared at her silently for a few seconds then gestured behind him to the door on the right. "Proceed," he said, as Damien landed in front of the last obstacle. Hally and Elowen looked at him briefly before opening the door and running through. It shut behind them with a resounding 'click' and they were faced with several mud ditches.

"No!" said Hally, angrily. "I know I got that right. Why has he put us on the hard obstacle course?"

The door opened again and Damien came through with a confused expression on his face. He saw them and said, "Well, I know I got that one wrong. What did you say it was?"

Hally huffed and turned away, so Elowen said, "A snowflake."

Damien frowned, "Well that makes more sense than what I said - a human."

Hally stomped her foot and said, "That's because we were right! He sent us through the wrong door!"

Damien frowned, but said, "There's no point in standing here complaining. We need to go. Come on!"

The next part of the obstacle course took them through the mud crawls and ditches, and the three moved through quickly using each other's help, exiting covered in mud from head to foot. Elowen spat mud out of her mouth and tried unsuccessfully to wipe her face clean. They were faced by another set of doors where a more friendly Shikari smiled and gave them a riddle - "What tastes better than it smells?" - which they answered correctly ("A tongue," said Hally.) and were led through the correct door this time.

Ahead of them, they found Mol and his partner balancing on a single-rope bridge holding a second rope, across more mud. He nodded at them, wobbled a little, leaning forward, then back, and causing his partner to wobble, too. Elowen, Damien and Hally waited until he was across then each proceeded to make their way as quickly as they could.

The forest around them was getting dark by the time they reached the final part of the obstacle course, which had wound its way back to the clearing and ended at the huge maze, the walls disappearing into the distance on the right and left. Through the tops of the trees, bright stars twinkled and the moonlight shone through into the maze. The high wooden walls of the maze stretched above them, touching the leaves of the tall conifers. Mol disappeared around a corner just as they entered the maze.

Hally, Elowen and Damien reached the first split leading left and right, and paused to catch their breath - all three were panting after the previous part of the course: walls and balancing beams. Elowen put her hands on her knees and drew in deep gulps of cold air, then looked at Hally questioningly.

"How do we know which way to go?" she asked breathlessly, straightening and rubbing her back. She had hoped Brannon would have followed her and advised her on directions from his vantage point above the maze. Where was he? she wondered.

Hally retrieved and unfolded a paper from a pocket in her tunic. It was worn and yellowing, and completely blank. She then proceeded to take some graphite and draw an arrow going in the same direction they had seen Mol disappear.

"Come on," she said quietly, as though not wanting to disturb the quiet of the maze. "We won't know which way to go unless we try, so we may as well not dawdle."

Elowen nodded and they turned and hurried down the path leading to the right. Turning another corner to the left, they came to another intersection.

Hally drew another arrow on the map leading to the left. They ran down several paths, twisting this way and that when suddenly they reached a dead end. Hally sighed and looked at the map again, then swore; it had gone completely blank.

"We must have gotten that wrong," said Damien.

Hally glared at him and said, "Thank you, genius." She looked at the map again. "I really thought this would work, but there must be some kind of magic that prevents us from tracing our steps."

Damien nodded and turned around to face the way they had just come. Elowen glanced around, too, as she heard him groan; the way split behind them into three paths.

"Now what," he asked. He ran his hand through his hair and his eyebrows were pinched in concern.

Elowen shrugged and replied, "I guess we go for the one on the extreme right."

"How do you know that?"

"I don't. I'm just guessing it would head toward the end because there's a turn ahead leading in that direction. I think," she added, hoping she was right.

Hally and Damien nodded and they jogged down the path. They followed it some way before reaching another split, which took them down another narrow path. This pattern continued for some time before they reached the centre of a four-way split.

Damien groaned and Hally let out a frustrated moan. Elowen felt suddenly lightheaded as her heart began to race in the realisation that they were completely lost, which was just as the maze would have it if it were 'alive' like the Marasae Labyrinth. The walls seemed to close in on them and she closed her eyes and pinched the bridge of her nose to calm the panic she was feeling. When she looked again, Hally was staring at her, concern etched on her face.

"You okay, El?" asked Damien, putting a hand on her shoulder.

"I don't know if I can do this," whispered Elowen. She had always found closed spaces scary, and this maze was beginning to feel endless. What if they never got out of this maze, let alone the Labyrinth? They'd be stuck there forever.

"You can do this," said Hally forcefully. "We're right here with you, okay? You are not alone."

Elowen nodded then took a deep breath. "This way, I think." She pointed down the path ahead of them and the three headed that way. They reached another dead end, retraced their steps and took the path to the left. They ran down a straight path for what felt like an age before it suddenly turned and they faced a small clearing surrounded by the thick forest. They had made it out, it seemed, but something felt... off. It was too quiet.

"This doesn't feel right," said Hally, her voice soft and cautious as she stepped past Elowen and faced the massive trees. It was dark, too dark to see past the thick trunks and the silence pressed on them with a heaviness until they felt claustrophobic and trapped.

"There's more than one exit?" asked Elowen, just as quietly.

"No, this is the exit, alright," she answered, "but we should not be alone. Where are Aavos and the other entrants?" She was about to turn when she suddenly stopped and reached inside her tunic for a dagger that was not there. Elowen glanced at Damien to find him focused rather on the trees, as though he had seen something. Then he gasped, stepping forward, and Elowen whipped her head around as something moved in the corner of her eye.

Out of the tree line stepped a man with silver hair, wearing a Shikari outfit. Just as relief began pouring into Elowen, she noticed something that made her freeze: he had pointed ears. This was no man - this was a Newid. Before she could begin backing away, the Newid pulled a bow and arrow from his back and took aim at Hally.

"No!" cried Elowen just as Hally shouted, "Run, El!"

Elowen did run - right in front of Hally as the Newid loosed the arrow. It flew at Hally's heart, but before it could reach its mark, Elowen was there, and the arrow pierced her shoulder, causing pain to shoot outward and, in agony, making Elowen scream.

But the pain didn't stop there. Another pain, not unlike the one she had been experiencing the night before, rippled out from her chest. It called to her with a familiarity, asking her to give in, but she screwed up her eyes and held onto the pain. She felt her body spasm in protest, but she kept her grip on the excruciating feeling, as though she knew what would happen if she gave in. She heard a growl and it was a moment before she realised it had come from her. She opened her eyes in surprise and saw Newid grinning from where he stood.

A small part of her knew what was happening and welcomed the thought, screaming to be let free, but another part of her resisted, shaking its head in stubbornness. Not now, not yet, it said. Then Elowen noticed something that almost had her let go of her control completely: there was a soft, purplish glow emanating from her. She felt a tickling in her ears and reached up to feel the tips suddenly pointed and unfamiliar. She felt a tingling in her fingertips and saw her nails grow sharp and claw-like.

She heard her name. "Elowen," the voice called, sounding distant. Hally. Elowen tried to pull herself together, knowing that if she didn't, the Change would keep happening.

"Elowen," another voice said. Damien. Her friends needed her.

But that was the wrong thought. In an instant, what looked like purplish-black tendrils of a thick and shiny liquid began weaving their way around and through Elowen so that it became impossible to tell where she began and where the magic ended. Then she was on all fours, a growl again ripping from her throat and echoing through the clearing. And she knew, without needing to look, that she was a massive beast, ready to protect, and kill.

Chapter 12

Captured

The smile on the Newid's face vanished and he stared at Elowen in shock and confusion. He began backing away so quickly that his feet caught on a stray tree root and he fell over. Elowen's legs trembled as she readied herself to pounce. The Newid scrambled to his feet and began to run, zigzagging from tree to tree, just as a second shiver ran down Elowen's spine. Pain shot through her again. Suddenly, the same tendrils lashed out from her and she found herself on hands and knees, panting as the pain left her with only a strange tingling in her arms and legs.

She took a deep breath, struggling to her feet, but gasped in pain as her shoulder began to throb. She looked down to find the arrow shaft sticking out of her shoulder and blood gushing out from the wound. Nausea roiled through her and she felt a rush of lightheadedness. Her legs gave way and she collapsed, just as strong arms reached out and grabbed her, laying her gently to the ground. She groaned, eyes fluttering, and tried to take a deep, shuddering breath. Elowen looked up to find Damien beside her, his face close to hers. He held her tightly, too tightly. She groaned again.

"Are you okay?" he murmured, his breath tickling her cheek. His dark eyes shone with concern and fear.

"You have nice eyes," she found herself whispering back, her thoughts muddled and her brain foggy. She felt her cheeks heat up as he chuckled, somewhat darkly. "Where's the Newid," she quickly added.

"Gone," came the voice of Hally somewhere behind Damien. "He vanished into the forest after you... well, whatever it was that you just did."

Elowen found herself searching for Hally's face and when she found it, she was surprised to see distrust and shock etched on it. Hally knelt down beside Elowen and Damien and looked down at the arrow sticking out of Elowen's shoulder.

She sighed and said, "Thank you for doing that for me though that was very stupid. We had better pull it out; your magic is already healing the wound around the arrowhead." She grabbed the arrow close to the head and looked at Elowen uncomfortably. "This will hurt, I'm sorry. I'll count to three: One... Two... THREE!" She yanked with all her might and the arrow was ripped out of Elowen's shoulder in seconds, causing Elowen to scream in pain.

"Sorry, sorry, sorry," said Hally, and she quickly chucked the arrow away. Elowen stared in amazement as she watched the flesh begin to knit itself back together.

Damien sat back and whistled in amazement. "Now, that's a neat trick."

Elowen looked around then. The forest was empty, though in a tree close by she spotted Brannon in the shape of a barn owl watching her closely. He nodded his head, his red eyes flashing, and took flight into the night sky.

"So," started Hally. "You want to tell us what just happened? Because that was no Newidian Change. That was something else entirely."

Elowen shrugged and struggled to her feet, Hally and Damien mimicking her movement. The three of them stood looking around the quiet clearing where it appeared nothing out of the ordinary had just happened. Elowen rubbed her face and eventually said, "I don't really understand what happened myself."

"Has that ever happened before?" asked Damien quietly.

"Yes, once, a long time ago." Elowen quickly told them the story.

Hally was frowning at Elowen and said, "I have never seen a Change like that before. It was not at all like how the Newids changed. It must be your magic."

Elowen nodded and replied, "It is mimicry magic."

"What's that?" asked Damien, frowning in confusion.

"It has to do with this." Elowen pulled out the Ornette, the ruby glinting in the moonlight. "It's an Ornette that contains the spirit of Brannon the Destroyer."

"What does it do?" asked Hally, leaning closer to examine the Ornette.

"It's supposed to control my powers and help me use them."

"And it contains Brannon the Destroyer?" Hally asked.

"Yes. When I attuned to the necklace, he revealed himself to me in his true form."

Damien and Hally exchanged a worried glance just as Brannon landed next to them, causing all three of them to jump back in fright. He ruffled his feathers impatiently and glared at them with his red eyes.

Aavos is on his way.

Damien and Hally both blinked in shock as Brannon's voice reverberated through their minds, too.

"Where have they all been?" asked Elowen, rubbing her shoulder gingerly; it had now begun to itch.

Fighting the other Newids who came to capture you.

"How many came?" asked Elowen, shocked.

Three have been captured by Aavos and the other entrants.

Hally bent forward to look at Brannon. She reached out a hand to touch him, as though not quite believing her eyes.

"What are you?" she whispered, eyes wide.

"I'll explain later," said Elowen, as, out of the maze, came Aavos. He looked livid but frowned in concern as he spotted Damien, Elowen and Hally.

"Are you three alright?" he said gruffly, looking around the clearing.

They nodded in unison and Hally stepped forward to tell Aavos what had happened, leaving out some details which would have told Aavos about Elowen's Change. Elowen glanced at Hally in surprise and gratitude.

"And he just ran away?" Aavos asked, shocked, then muttered to himself, "Why didn't he just attack? Well, come on, you three. Let's get back to the rest of the class. It will be quicker to go through the maze."

Elowen yawned widely and followed Aavos back into the maze, Hally and Damien walking close behind her. It took them a short amount of time to make their way through the maze to where the other entrants were gathered - Aavos seemed to know precisely where to go.

Once they had all gathered, Aavos began directing the other Shikari to take the captured Newids back to Pamor Tower. The three Newids, all with the same pointed ears as Gundrel stared at Elowen with a mixture of fury and hurt, even as they were shoved away by the Shikari holding them captive. Once they had left, Aavos led them to the main clearing where they had been practising and where there now lay many bed rolls for them to sleep for the night.

Damien, Hally and Elowen quickly grabbed three bed rolls and pulled them to the edge of the clearing where they would be out of earshot from the rest of the entrants, who also grabbed their bed rolls and began laying down for the night. Elowen, Hally and Damien lay down, too, Elowen in the middle, and began whispering to one another.

"That was insane," started Hally. She lay leaning on her elbow facing Elowen and Damien. "I want to know what happened to you, Elowen."

Elowen nodded, lifting herself by her elbows, and said, "I believe I have mimic magic."

"Yes, you said that, but what does that mean?" asked Damien, his chin resting on his hand as he, too, faced Elowen and Hally.

Elowen pursed her lips, thinking. She took a deep breath, then said, "I don't really know that much, but I will share with you what Brannon told me. I am a mimic; I can change into any creature. I am not limited to just one animal, like the Newids."

"That's why Gundrel was so shocked when he saw you change," said Hally quietly. "He assumed you would change as Newid changes, but it looked as though you used magic. And I assume he thought you would change into a wolf, not a bear."

"That's what I changed into?"

You didn't know?" Hally started, shocked. "Surely you wanted to change into a bear or you were thinking of changing into a bear?"

"No, I just remember thinking I needed to protect you two, and then I changed."

Silence followed, broken by the occasional hoot of an owl or chirp of a cricket. Damien frowned and eventually said, "You mentioned that the Ornette focuses your powers and contains a soul-"

"Souls, actually."

Hally looked appalled and said, "What do you mean?"

Elowen quickly told them what Brannon had told her about her grandmother creating the Ornette. "It contains the souls of six Newids, to focus my powers better."

"This sounds wrong, Elowen. I think you should take it off. Where did you get it anyway?"

"From Mistress Monige, or Imogen, and I cannot take it off, or destroy it, for that matter. I've tried."

"Mistress Monige gave that to you?" Hally's eyebrows disappeared behind her fringe. "This is making less sense the more you tell us. I thought the mistress was trying to save you from your grandmother, but now she's giving you gifts from that same grandmother?"

Elowen paused as she thought this through. Hally had a point; why had she received this Ornette from her grandmother if she was hiding from her? She yawned widely and rubbed her eyes, which felt like they had weights pressing down on them. Shaking her head, she said, "I don't know much else besides that."

"And what about Brannon the Destroyer?"

"He was also a mimic, and he binds the souls of the other Newids."

"And now he's, what, your pet?" said Hally, snorting quietly.

"No, he's supposed to help me-"

"He sounds dangerous to me," piped up Damien. "If this Ornette is meant to help you control your powers, why weren't you able to control them earlier? You were barely transformed for more than a couple of seconds at most, Elowen."

Elowen paused and thought. Things definitely weren't adding up and she was starting to feel quite nervous. She gave the Ornette another tug as though it would suddenly come free this time. Elowen glanced at Hally and found concern and worry etched upon her face.

Hally sighed and lay down, shifting around in her bed roll to get comfortable. "El, we need to get that Ornette off. I can't imagine what Imogen was thinking when she gave it to you, but it's wrong."

"What if it's a Coven of the Dark thing that we just don't understand?"

"I think," started Damien again, "that we should do some reading on this. There must be a book somewhere in Pamor Library about Brannon the Destroyer and mimics."

Hally nodded and said, "And Ornettes that contain souls. Just, don't trust it."

She stopped talking suddenly as a black shape darted out of the sky and landed beside them. Brannon transformed into a massive black dog that lay down at Elowen's head.

I did a search of the perimeter. You're safe, mistress.

Elowen frowned and glanced at Brannon. "I don't understand what happened earlier; where were you? You could have warned us about Gundrel and the other Newids, but you didn't."

My apologies, I did not see them in time. They were well hidden, mistress.

Hally turned to exchange a look with Elowen. Her eyebrow was raised and she looked disbelieving. Even Damien pursed his lips and lay down so that a silence stretched an uncomfortable, stressful silence.

Elowen bit her lip and frowned. She opened her mouth to speak, closed it, then opened it again and eventually said, "Did you see where Gundrel went?"

No, mistress.

"Please call me Elowen."

No, Elowen. Would you like me to follow his tracks for you?

Elowen thought about it and was about to answer 'yes' when Hally suddenly said, "I don't think there's much use in doing that. I think we should think about speaking to the Newids they have captured. Let's get to sleep. We can head to the library tomorrow morning."

"Don't we have training tomorrow?"

"Yes, but only in the afternoon do we need to head to class. We have the morning off."

Elowen nodded and turned onto her side. The ground was hard beneath her and she shifted this way and that before falling into a fitful sleep. Her sleep was scattered with unusual dreams that had her waking after each one, opening her eyes to find, with surprise, that she was sleeping beneath the stars.

She was just drifting off again when she heard a rustling through the trees close to their bedrolls and a low growl from Brannon reached her ears. Her eyes shot open and she shifted her head slightly to catch Brannon's eye.

Go back to sleep, Elowen.

"What did you hear?" she asked softly, shifting onto her stomach and elbows. She squinted into the night, the dark shadows from the trees playing tricks on her mind; was one of them moving?

Brannon stood and took a step toward one of the shadows and in an instant, the shadow shifted and two eyes stared at them. Two Newid eyes. Gundrel held up his hands placatingly, then did something most unexpected: he bowed.

Elowen's eyes widened and she sat up suddenly. She almost reached over to wake Hally, but Gundrel took a step forward and shook his head.

"Wait," he whispered. "Please, I must speak with you."

Elowen frowned, shimmied out of her bedroll and stood up. She made her way to Gundrel, walking tall to hide how nervous she was. "You had every chance to speak with me before you shot an arrow at me."

"I shot an arrow at the Shikari girl," snapped Gundrel, a little too loudly. Hally shifted slightly in her bedroll, then turned over and carried on snoring. Gundrel took a placating breath and then said, "I'm so sorry, princess. I only came to rescue you."

Brannon prowled to Elowen's side, eyes narrowed and focused on Gundrel. Gundrel glanced at Brannon, confused, but said nothing. Instead, he bowed again and took a tentative step toward Elowen.

"I cannot remain for long, but please hear me out. Those Newids who were captured were only doing their job to your father. Help them. You belong with us, Elowen. You are a Newid and you need training. Please, you don't have to decide now but think it through. Your power will consume you if you don't learn to control it."

Elowen felt a shiver of fear run down her spine as she considered his words. A part of her really wanted to go with Gundrel and meet her father, but what about her promise to Darwin and Gavin and Imogen? She also did not yet know if she could trust this Newid. In fact, there was very little she felt she knew in general and felt she had very few people she knew she could trust. Things just weren't adding up and she needed to do some research into it. She opened her mouth to answer Gundrel, but Gundrel's eyes shifted to a spot somewhere behind her and widened, then he took a cautious step back, then another one.

"We will see each other again soon, princess. Think it over. I will find you"

Then he was gone, and Elowen was left standing feeling alone and confused. Brannon looked up at her, then prowled away to his original spot.

Let's sleep, Elowen.

Elowen made her way back to her bedroll and climbed in, savouring the warmth and cosiness. She sighed. She had so much to consider and work out - it was all so overwhelming.

She turned over toward Damien and found his eyes open and searching hers. He gave her a small smile, then reached over with his hand to take hers. Closing his eyes, he said, "We'll look into everything tomorrow. Don't worry."

So Elowen closed her eyes, trying hard to ignore the worry that clawed at her heart and fell back to sleep.

Chapter 13

Visit to the Library

The next morning dawned bright and fresh as the entrants packed up and began to prepare themselves to go back to Pamor Tower. Everyone was groggy-eyed and moody, the night had been a restless and uncomfortable one, and no one spoke as they rolled up their bedrolls and gathered their things. There was a great sigh of relief when Aavos suggested they go a shorter and quicker route to get back to Pamor Tower.

Elowen, Damien, and Hally set out from the clearing ahead of the others, walking towards Pamor Tower through the suffocatingly dense forest. The hike back seemed to take no time at all. The quiet of the forest pressed in on them. As they ventured into the heart of the lush forest, their senses came alive with a symphony of sounds and a kaleidoscope of sights. The air was thick with the earthy scent of damp moss and the fragrance of wildflowers, enticing their every breath. The towering canopy above filtered the golden sunlight, casting mesmerising patterns of dappled light and shadow upon the forest floor. The rustling leaves created a gentle chorus, accompanied by the soft murmur of a babbling brook, weaving a soothing melody. Birdsong filled the air, a harmonious blend of chirping, trilling, and melodic calls, as colourful feathered creatures flitted between branches, their vibrant plumage painting the forest with flashes of emerald, ruby, and sapphire. Squirrels scampered and played, their nimble movements adding playful energy to the scene, while the occasional scurrying of unseen creatures hinted at the hidden life that thrived beneath the undergrowth.

Elowen led the way, her sharp purple eyes scanning the forest for any signs of danger, while Damien walked beside her, his hand resting on the hilt of a sword he'd picked up from Aavos on their way out. Hally trailed behind, the backpack she had carried to the clearing yesterday bouncing on her shoulders as she hummed a tune to herself. As they walked, they found themselves dodging several obstacles, from fallen trees to a small stream that they had to wade through. But they pressed on, their determination unwavering.

Above them, Brannon flew above the trees in the form of a black falcon, keeping watch from up high. Elowen found herself distracted by his ominous form and kept glancing his way, hoping he would disappear. She was growing more and more worried the more she thought of him and the Ornette. She hoped they would find something in the library about it to put her mind at ease.

After several hours of walking, they finally caught sight of the Pamor Tower, rising tall and proud against the skyline. The Sea of Apias glittered behind it. The sight filled them with renewed energy, and they quickened their pace, eager to reach their destination.

They eventually hurried into the Tower, but while the rest of the entrants went to breakfast, Elowen, Hally and Damien made their way to the library at the top of the tower. Brannon, transformed into a small mouse, nestled himself in Elowen's pocket. They stepped into the grand room, built with shimmering white marble and adorned with intricate carvings depicting creatures and celestial constellations, and their eyes widened in awe at the sight of the towering shelves filled with ancient tomes and dusty scrolls. The shelves, crafted from rare enchanted woods, stretched as far as the eye could see, housing thousands of books, scrolls, and manuscripts. The air was filled with the scent of aged parchment and ink, and a soft, ambient glow emanated from floating orbs that hovered throughout the space, providing ample illumination for readers. Comfortable reading nooks with plush armchairs were interspersed among the shelves, providing cosy corners for reading and relaxing. The library was strangely empty, save for the librarian who took a determined step toward them.

"Welcome to Pamor Tower library," said the stern-looking librarian with glasses perched on the tip of her nose. Clad in flowing robes adorned with intricate patterns and symbols, she eyed them warily as though worried they had gotten lost. Then she began talking, as though reciting something, "The library is divided into distinct sections, each dedicated to a different branch of knowledge. The Hall of Legends holds tomes that chronicle the heroic deeds and mythical creatures of the realm, from ancient dragons to valiant knights. The Chamber of Arcana houses a collection of spellbooks and grimoires, their pages filled with incantations, rituals, and the secrets of magic.

"For those seeking to understand the natural world, the Whispering Gardens section offers a vast selection of botanical volumes and zoological encyclopaedias, their pages filled with descriptions of fantastic flora and fauna found in the realm. Alchemical laboratories adjacent to this section allow scholars to experiment with rare ingredients and concoct potent elixirs.

"The Labyrinth of History contains countless volumes detailing the rise and fall of civilizations, legends of forgotten realms, and the tales of ancient artefacts. The space is adorned with tapestries depicting key historical events, and ancient relics and artefacts are displayed in glass cases, showcasing the wonders of bygone eras.

"At the heart of the library lies the Celestial Observatory, a domed chamber with a crystalline roof that allows scholars to study the stars and decipher the secrets of the cosmos. Here, astronomers and astrologers pore over ancient star charts and celestial manuscripts, seeking knowledge of the heavens and the threads that connect them to the realm below."

The librarian stopped talking and stared at them expectantly. Elowen felt slightly overwhelmed by the sudden onslaught of information and glanced at Hally and Damien, unsure.

Damien approached the librarian and asked for books on shapeshifting. The librarian led them to a section filled with books on magic and supernatural abilities, and they began to peruse the titles. Damien pulled out a large tome titled "The Art of Shapeshifting," and they settled down at a nearby table to read it. The book was filled with detailed illustrations and instructions on how to control one's shapeshifting abilities, from mastering the transformation to maintaining the altered form.

"This is perfect," said Elowen, clapping her hands together and began to read:

In the Land of Mid-Eberra, shapeshifting is a rare but powerful ability possessed by a select few. Those who possess this ability can transform their physical form into that of any creature or object they can imagine. Shapeshifting can be used for a variety of purposes, from stealth and deception to combat and exploration. However, it comes with a great cost, as each transformation taxes the shapeshifter's physical and mental stamina. Some shapeshifters are born with this ability, while others acquire it through exposure to magic or other supernatural forces. Those who discover their shapeshifting abilities must learn to control them while navigating the dangers and complexities of a world where shapeshifters are both feared and coveted.

Elowen shook her head and skipped ahead a few pages.

Shapeshifting abilities are typically portrayed as powerful and uncontrollable, often leading to chaos and destruction. However, if one were to possess such abilities, it would be important to learn how to control them. The first step in controlling shapeshifting abilities is to gain a deep understanding of the triggers that initiate the transformation. By identifying these triggers, such as emotions, thoughts, or physical sensations, one can learn to manage and prevent them. Additionally, practising meditation and mindfulness can help to maintain focus and control over the shapeshifting abilities. It is also important to develop a strong sense of self and personal identity, as shapeshifting can blur the lines between oneself and others. Finally, seeking out guidance and support from others with similar abilities can help master and control shapeshifting abilities.

Elowen smiled and said, "This is great." She began turning to another page when she felt a small movement in her pocket; Brannon. She had almost forgotten about him. Elowen looked around and spotted the librarian. Quickly closing the book and leaving Hally and Damien to peruse their chosen books, she went to the librarian.

The librarian looked up from the book she was reading and considered Elowen curiously. "May I help you, dear?" she asked quietly.

"I was wondering if you had any books on Ornettes?"

The librarian nodded and stood, motioning Elowen to follow her. She led the way through towering bookshelves, turning so many corners Elowen began to feel lost. Deeper they made their way into the silence of the library, where fewer orbs glowed, casting greater shadows over the books. Eventually, they stopped at a section and the librarian pulled a book from the shelf, handing it to Elowen. Then the librarian disappeared round a corner, leaving Elowen in the stifling silence, feeling very alone and nervous.

Elowen opened the book to the first page and was surprised to find the book to be a very old one. It had illumination art that in itself was absolutely stunning and distracting, so much so that Elowen found herself staring at the art in wonder for some time before remembering she needed to read. She shook her head and read the first page quickly.

The Ornette is a truly extraordinary necklace, possessing an enchanting power that surpasses the imagination. Adorned with intricate designs and glistening gemstones, this remarkable accessory bestows upon its wearer the extraordinary ability to control and harness the mystical art of shapeshifting. When worn, the Ornette unlocks a realm of limitless transformation, granting the individual the power to alter their physical form at will. With a mere thought, one can seamlessly shift from one creature to another, transcending the boundaries of species and defying the laws of nature. The Ornette becomes a conduit for boundless self-expression and unparalleled adaptability, empowering its possessor to navigate through any situation with unparalleled grace and versatility.

However, while a powerful conduit, the Ornette can be created to withhold power. In rare cases, the Ornette will stop the wearer from being able to use their shapeshifting abilities, for the safety of those around it. It is therefore imperative to understand that Ornettes cannot be trusted to provide more power when, in fact, they can withhold power from the wearer.

Elowen frowned and proceeded to turn to the next page. It was at that moment that she became aware of Brannon moving in her pocket and she looked down, almost shrieking in fright as a black snake began slithering out of her pocket and onto her shoulders.

What are you looking for, Elowen, that I cannot tell you directly?

Elowen scowled and said, "It seems you haven't been completely honest with me about this Ornette."

How so? Brannon seemed to hiss in her ear as though insulted that she would question him.

Elowen read the paragraph she had just read out loud for Brannon and then said, "That would explain why I wasn't able to stay transformed for very long."

Brannon sighed, a strange hissing sound that had Elowen cringing. *It was impressive that you were able to turn at all if I am to be completely honest. The Ornette was supposed to control your powers completely and prevent you from turning at all. It seems you are more powerful than Imogen anticipated.*

"Imogen knew that the Ornette would do this?"

Of course. She was the one who designed and made it. Not your grandmother or mother. She had hoped it would protect you and those around you. I did not agree, but then, what could I have done to stop her?

Elowen's mind reeled and her heart raced. Imogen had tried to stop her transformations. Again, Elowen tried to take the Ornette off, but to no avail. She quickly flipped through the book, looking for any information that might suggest how to get the necklace off.

I was not able to stop her trying to control you, but I might be able to help you get the Ornette off. If you would like my help, of course.

"I thought I was attuned to this Ornette?" whispered Elowen, almost to herself. She was feeling extremely anxious that she would never get the necklace off.

Yes, you'll need to stop attuning, but because this Ornette was created so that you cannot take it off, you will need to destroy it.

"I've already tried that, remember? It didn't work."

You cannot destroy it with normal objects like knives. You must use a magically imbued object.

"Okay, where do I find that?"

You will need to go through the Tenebris and the Passage.

Elowen frowned. "The Passage.... I've heard that before. Isn't that the place that connects parts of this world to make it easier to traverse?"

Indeed. There are parts of this world only accessible through the Passage. There is one place, a trove of treasures, that has what you are looking for a magically imbued dagger known as the Carver.

Elowen nodded and said, "How do I get there?"

There is an Entrance in the Marasae Labyrinth. Part of your trial is to navigate the Labyrinth and enter the Passage. You will be able to find the door to this trove of treasures but you will be required to answer a riddle of sorts.

Elowen groaned. "Not another riddle." She sighed and put the book back into its place. "What is it with this world and riddles?"

It was believed to be the true test of intellect.

Elowen turned and began making her way back to Hally and Damien. It took some time to find the correct way back as she kept taking wrong turns and getting lost, but eventually, she rounded the corner to find Damien and Hally lounging in their seats waiting for her. They glanced at Brannon in shock and distaste but quickly masked their expressions with a smile. Elowen sat down at the table and pulled a book towards her.

"Where did you go?" asked Damien, leaning forward.

"I found a book on Ornettes." She quickly filled them in on what she had read and what Brannon had told her. "I'd like to find this room."

Hally nodded slowly, glancing at Brannon quickly before looking away. "We can do that."

Elowen nodded and was about to turn to the book in front of her when movement out of the corner of her eye drew her attention away from Hally and Damien. She felt Brannon suddenly shift and disappear into her pocket.

"Elowen?"

Elowen blinked in surprise. Lord Gimrad was standing at an open door in the middle of some bookshelves. It looked like the door to a hidden room. Damien and Hally looked up in surprise, too, and exchanged a glance with Elowen. Elowen stood up quickly, slamming the book shut with finality. Lord Gimrad beckoned them to follow him through the door.

Elowen hesitated for a second, then pushed herself forward through the door. They entered a spacious and expensive study that was adorned with elegant decor. It featured a combination of soothing colours of soft greys, muted blues and warm earth tones and the walls had stunning artwork along it. The focal point was a long sleek desk made of polished wood, complemented by large leather chairs, one behind the desk and five in front of the desk. Along the walls, there were bookshelves stocked with a diverse range of reference books, textbooks, and literary classics. An orb glowed above the desk providing warmth and light to the room.

Seated in two of the chairs were two men who looked up expectantly when Elowen, Damien and Hally entered. They smiled, though neither smile reached their eyes. They were both very large and had long black hair and eyes. They looked almost identical, except for the long scar across the one's face. They both seemed relaxed, though Elowen could not help but notice the large number of knives adorning their Shikari outfits. They, too, wore Shikari badges that shone in the light of the orb.

"Please, sit," said Lord Gimrad as he made his way behind the desk and sat down facing the five chairs.

Elowen, Damien and Hally sat down reluctantly, though curiously; why had they been called into this apparent meeting?

"Elowen, Hally, Damien, I'd like to introduce you to Lupus and Chete." Lord Gimrad indicated the two men seated at the table. Both men nodded at them then turned back expectantly to Lord Gimrad.

"We are in a hurry, you'll remember," said the one with the scar.

"Yes, Lupus. I have not forgotten the mission from which I called you, but please bear with me as I fill them in."

"What's going on, father," asked Damien, frowning.

Lord Gimrad glanced at Damien and sighed, a little impatiently, as though not keen to be called 'father' in front of Chete and Lupus.

"I heard about your run-in with Gundrel yesterday," he started, looking concernedly at Elowen and even glancing at her shoulder as if he knew she had been shot. "I want to apologise for not being there." He looked at Damien briefly, who nodded. "I'd also like to make sure that you are all okay?"

Hally glanced at Elowen, then said, rather brazenly, "What is it that you need of us?"

Lord Gimrad shifted in his seat and then said, "I need you," he looked at Elowen seriously, "to transform."

Chapter 14

A Mission

Elowen blanched. She had not been expecting to hear that. Her heart started pounding and a bead of sweat trickled down her forehead; it was feeling excessively stuffy in this room all of a sudden. She shook her head and felt a hand rest on her arm as though to steady her. Hally gave her a small, encouraging smile.

"I can't," Elowen blurted out and she shifted uncomfortably under everyone's glaze.

"Well, it doesn't have to be right now-"

"No, I can't at all. This," she lifted the Ornette out from under her shirt, "prevents me from transforming."

"An Ornette," said Lupus, surprised. "Where did you get that?"

"It was... a gift," Elowen said, not wanting to give away too much information to this new man.

"Why do you need her to transform, father?" said Damien quietly, frowning.

Lord Gimrad sighed and looked at Chete and Lupus. "We have received word that the Newids intend to go to war with us soon and we were hoping we could get some inside information on what they plan on doing."

"Is there no way we can destroy this Ornette?" asked Chete leaning forward to look past Lupus at Elowen.

"Well, actually," started Elowen, "I think I know how to destroy this."

"You do?" said Lord Gimrad, surprised. "How?"

"I need to find a room in the Passage, which I can do during the Tournament."

Lord Gimrad nodded then said, "And once it's destroyed, we can start on our real mission."

"Which is?" asked Elowen nervously.

"You are going to infiltrate the Newids."

Silence followed Lord Gimrad's words. He continued, "We have been trying to infiltrate them for years and learn more about them. Now that we have learned, thanks to Lupus and Chete, that they wish to attack us, we need a Shikari to get inside information on their plans."

"But, I'm not Shikari yet," said Elowen reluctantly.

"You will be in a few days after you complete the Labyrinth. I have complete faith in the three of you."

"The three of us?" repeated Damien, surprised. "You mean for me to go with them?"

"Yes, you will go with Hally and Elowen and help them get to this trove where they will find the Carver. For the three of you, your focus will be on getting rid of that Ornette. Then, once you have done that, you will swear into being a Shikari and then your first mission will start."

"What exactly do you expect from me?" asked Elowen quietly. She was feeling both excited and a little nervous.

Lord Gimrad answered, "First, you will gather information, researching the Newids extensively, including their history, culture, known members, weaknesses and vulnerabilities that could be exploited, and you will identify key individuals who might have valuable information or influence. You'll need to establish a cover story and build connections by attending gatherings, events or festivals, and you should find potential allies. Next, you will need to hone your shapeshifting abilities by finding a mentor or teacher who can help you develop your powers. You will also need to gain entry to restricted areas that hold valuable information or secrets, acquire intel and evidence and share it with us. Any questions so far?"

Elowen's mind was reeling from the onslaught of information. She wracked her brain for any questions and eventually asked, "How will I get there?"

"I'm glad you asked," said Lord Gimrad, smiling. "We are fortunate to have Newids that we have captured. You will earn their trust and help free them and they will take you to their home."

Elowen nodded slowly, then glanced at Hally, who had remained very quiet. Hally grimaced then said, "How will we be allowed to come with the Newids?"

"I don't think you will be," said Lord Gimrad. "You will need to follow Elowen from a distance and not get caught. Now then, about the Marasae Tournament, you will need to focus on physical conditioning, problem-solving, obstacle course training, maze navigation, and mental resilience. The rest of this week you will need to train the hardest you have ever trained. Do you think you could do that?"

Elowen glanced at Hally and Damien and then nodded along with them. She had been training for this her whole life; she felt ready.

"Good, then I suggest you go make some headway with the Newids while I finish up my meeting with Lupus and Chete. The guards are on a shift change now so you should be able to see the Newids without the guards stopping you. You'll have to be quick, though."

Hally, Damien and Elowen stood up and left the room, the secret door closing behind them with a resounding thump.

The walk down to the dungeons seemed to take no time at all. They climbed down the ladder descending into the depths of the dungeon, and the air grew heavier and the sounds of despair echoed through the narrow corridors.

The dungeon was a labyrinth of dimly lit passages and cold, damp cells. The walls, coated in layers of grime and decay, seemed to whisper of the suffering of those within. Rusty iron bars formed the confines of the cells, serving as a cruel reminder of the helplessness of the captives. Elowen shivered as a cool wind swept in through the open windows and she glanced at Hally and Damien in trepidation. They both nodded toward the first prison where a female Newid stood staring out the window. She wore black clothing and her long hair was a tangled mess, but she held herself with a proudness and calm that did not fit the prison she was in.

"We'll wait for you outside," whispered Hally as she took Damien by the arm and led him back out of the dungeons. Elowen was left wondering what she could possibly say to this Newid. She took a deep breath of cold air and made her way to the first prison.

"What do you want?" rasped the Newid, barely turning to look at Elowen.

Heart pounding, Elowen replied, "Sorry to bother you -"

The Newid choked out a laugh. "Bother me? What important tasks could you be disturbing me from?" She turned and gave Elowen a curious look. Then she looked away again and said, "You are not bothering me, child. Now, what do you want?"

Elowen sighed and said, "I am Elowen Farrowspire -"

"I know who you are. You are the reason I'm here."

Elowen frowned, bristling, and said, "That doesn't seem fair. You are here because you chose to come after me. If you had just let me know ahead of time that you were coming I might have been able to help you. So don't blame me for your poor choices."

Silence followed her words and the Newid turned to look at her again. "I suppose you are right. But that still doesn't change the fact that I am here."

"I'm here to help."

"How do you expect to help me? And how do you expect me to trust your help?"

Elowen thought and eventually replied, "The Shikari think I am on their side."

"Aren't you? It seems very clear you have chosen them over us."

Elowen shook her head and said, "I'm on nobody's side but my own. I want to help you escape so that you can take me to my father."

"The Shikari want you to spy on us," said the Newid wisely.

"Yes, they do."

"Then that is what you will have to do, to stay on their side."

Elowen nodded. "Helping you escape will be easy as they want it to happen."

"You should still do it on the night of the Tournament when there will be a huge party in honour of the entrants and Shikari."

Elowen thought about this and then smiled. "You've already planned this, haven't you? How did you know I'd come?"

The Newid paused before saying, "I didn't. I trusted Gundrel to have a plan. Did he speak to you?"

"Yes, he did. He wanted me to help you."

"He has a lot of faith in you, then. Fine, I will let you help the three of us escape in exchange for us taking you and only you to your home and father."

"Thank you," murmured Elowen, relief flooding through her.

"Freya. My name is Freya. And the Newids behind you are Tern and Jim," Elowen glanced into the cell behind her and was surprised to see two male Newids almost hidden in the shadows of the cell. They nodded in her direction.

"See you on the night of the Tournament, then," said Freya and she turned away.

The door to the dungeon opened and three guards made their way inside. Elowen quickly slipped past them. The guards gave her a curious glance but said nothing as she made her way outside.

Damien and Hally were standing off to the side waiting for her and when Elowen appeared, they quickly made their way over to her.

"Did you manage to convince them?" asked Hally and she grinned and patted Elowen on the shoulder when Elowen nodded. "Well done.

They must be desperate or they wouldn't have agreed so quickly or easily. "

Elowen chuckled and said, "Or I'm just very convincing." She sighed and glanced around. "It'll happen on the eve of the Tournament."

Damien nodded. "That makes sense. Everyone will be celebrating."

They began making their way upstairs to the dormitory. The rest of the entrants all lounged about talking about the events of the previous day. Hally, Damien and Elowen claimed a sofa away from the other entrants and began talking in hushed tones.

"I say we drug the guards," murmured Elowen, and Hally and Damien nodded.

"Simple, but effective, I'd say," said Hally. "A sleeping draught should be relatively quick and easy to make."

"Have you ever made it before?" asked Damien.

"Yes, once," replied Hally. "I'll start on it tonight and it should be ready in time. You, El, will need to focus on your training."

Elowen nodded and sighed. "The tournament is still a few days away. That should be plenty of time to train."

Damien smiled and said, "I don't want to be negative, but when I did the tournament last year, I also thought I was ready."

Elowen grimaced. "Oh goodness, don't say that."

"Sorry, but I don't believe anyone can ever be truly ready for the Tournament."

Hally shrugged and said, "He's not wrong. It is a hard Tournament. But you'll do your best and I'll do the rest."

Elowen tried to smile but her hammering heart made her swallow nervously instead.

"If I'm honest, I just need to get to the place where I can disable this Ornette. Everything else will just have to fall into place."

Damien nodded and reached out to pat Elowen's hand comfortingly. "I'm sure you'll be fine. You'll have us to help you."

"Thanks, Damien," said Elowen quietly, her heart suddenly hammering for a different reason.

"Well, I need to go to the store room to pick up ingredients for the draught," said Hally, getting up and making her way out of the room, leaving Damien and Elowen staring at each other. Elowen blushed and looked away, before saying, "So what is happening today."

Damien smiled and said, "Training."

And so, for the rest of the day, Damien and Elowen, along with the other entrants, all made their way to the massive training gym on one of the upper floors of Pamor Tower. There were many different parts to the gym with many different levels where you could practise or train.

Damien and Elowen spent most of the afternoon fighting each other, with many of the entrants stopping to watch them. They stood in the fighting ring circling each other. Elowen wasted no time, darting forward with lightning speed, a blur of motion. She struck with a flurry of acrobatic kicks and quick punches, testing Damien's defences. But Damien was no pushover. He deftly parried Elowen's attacks, showing off his impeccable reflexes. It was like a dance, one that Elowen was thoroughly enjoying. Elowen shifted her strategy, relying on her finesse and unpredictability. She spun gracefully, delivering precise strikes from unexpected angles. Damien, undeterred, met her movements with calculated counters, demonstrating his honed martial prowess. Both Elowen and Damien were breathing heavily, each knowing that the outcome hinged on this crucial moment. Elowen's eyes gleamed with determination, and Damien's jaw tightened with resolve.

The crowd erupted into cheers as the fighters clashed once more, their moves faster and more ferocious than ever before. Elowen's agility kept her just out of Damien's reach, while Damien's strength threatened to overpower her at every turn.

In a last-ditch effort, Damien unleashed a mighty strike, but Elowen saw an opening. She twisted gracefully, countering his attack with a perfectly timed sweep that sent Damien sprawling to the ground. The crowd gasped in awe at her skilful move.

With Damien temporarily disarmed, Elowen showed her sportsmanship by offering him a hand to get back on his feet. The two exchanged nods of respect, acknowledging each other's prowess.

With the fight over, Elowen decided to practise knife throwing and archery. She was good at both skills, hitting the target's centre nearly every time. Hally eventually reappeared toward the end of training with the good news that she had managed to get hold of all the necessary ingredients for the sleeping draught and the three of them made their way to dinner in the dining hall.

As the sun dipped below the horizon, casting a warm golden glow upon the hall, anticipation filled the air. The aroma of delectable delights wafted through the room, enticing every Shikari and entrant with its tantalising allure. The feast was about to begin.

Each table was adorned with intricate linens and sparkling silverware. Each place setting was meticulously arranged, with delicate porcelain plates and polished silver cutlery.

The feast showcased a kaleidoscope of flavours. The tantalising scent of freshly baked bread filled the air, while platters of succulent roasted meats took centre stage. Their rich, savoury aromas mingled with the delicate perfume of aromatic spices, enticing the taste buds and promising an unforgettable experience.

A colourful array of vibrant, seasonal vegetables burst forth from elegant serving bowls. Steamed asparagus spears, roasted root vegetables, and buttery baby carrots offered a delightful harmony of textures and flavours. Accompanying them were bowls of creamy mashed potatoes, golden-brown roasted potatoes, and fragrant rice, each prepared with the utmost care.

The feast boasted an impressive seafood selection, showcasing the ocean's treasures. Luscious platters of freshly shucked oysters, succulent lobster tails, and tender grilled salmon, perfectly seared to perfection, were presented with artistic flair. The seafood selection was further enhanced with a variety of dipping sauces, citrus-infused butter, and zesty lemon wedges.

A dazzling array of pastries, cakes, and sweet treats tantalised the eyes and beckoned to the sweet tooth within. Velvety chocolate truffles adorned with edible gold leaf, and sumptuous fruit tarts bursting with seasonal flavours delighted the senses. The air was alive with the scents of vanilla, cinnamon, and freshly brewed coffee.

Accompanying the feast are an array of fine wines, aged spirits, and refreshing beverages. The clinking of glasses and the soft murmur of conversation filled the room as guests savoured each bite, exchanging smiles and compliments on the food before them.

As the feast reached its crescendo, laughter and merriment resounded throughout the hall, and Master Gimrad made his way to the middle platform where he immediately grabbed everyone's attention and commanded silence to spread across the hall.

Once everyone was quiet, he said, "I have some exciting news everyone." He paused as he looked around the hall and his eyes caught Elowen's. "The Shikari have been discussing the Tournament and its timing and we have concluded that the Tournament will no longer take place in a week's time." There was confused murmuring and looks of outrage on most entrant's faces. "It will take place tomorrow."

Chapter 15

The Tournament

The wind howled through the trees, whipping fallen leaves through the air and battering the horseback riders as they made their way through the forest surrounding the Labyrinth. Anticipation and worry hung in the air around the entrants and none of them spoke, too nervous to even ask how much longer they would be riding for. They had been riding since early that morning, before the birds had even begun to wake, and though they knew they couldn't be far now, not one of them dared ask for fear that they would bring the Tournament to a start.

The news they had received last night regarding the Tournament had brought cries of outrage and fear from the entrants.

"But we were meant to have training for the rest of the week," many of them had yelled as Master Gimrad had raised his hands placatingly.

"Calm yourselves, my fellow future Shikari!" Master Gimrad had shouted over the din. "It is time to celebrate, not protest; we have deemed you ready for the Tournament in a way that no other entrants have been deemed ready. You should be proud of yourselves and congratulate yourselves on being such excellent candidates for this Tournament. I have no doubt you will all pass with flying colours."

With those words still hanging in the air the following day, Elowen shifted on her horse to get comfortable just as the Labyrinth came into view.

Nestled within the heart of the serene, enchanted forest, the Marasae Labyrinth stood as an architectural marvel, beckoning all who dared to embark on a journey of wonder. The captivating labyrinth blended seamlessly with the lush, natural surroundings.

As the entrants approached the entrance to the Labyrinth, a sense of anticipation and intrigue washed over them. Two towering, moss-covered stone pillars guarded the gateway to the Marasae Labyrinth, their ancient carvings hinting at the mysteries that lay within. Worn steps, bearing the footprints of countless seekers, led the way into the labyrinth's depths.

Once inside, the labyrinth unveiled itself as a harmonious fusion of artistry and nature. A verdant canopy of ancient trees, their branches interwoven to form a living ceiling, cast dappled sunlight upon the intricate paths below. The cool, earthy scent of the forest mingled with the delicate fragrance of wildflowers that graced the labyrinth's edges, creating a sensory symphony that enchanted the soul.

The labyrinth's meandering pathways were meticulously laid with smooth, worn cobblestones, their intricate designs weaving stories of generations of wanderers who had tread its ground. Along the way, hidden nooks and niches sheltered delicate statues of mythical creatures, their weathered forms whispering tales of guardianship and guidance.

As they ventured deeper into the labyrinth, the gentle murmur of a crystal-clear stream grew louder. Suddenly, the path opened into a breathtaking central plaza. There, a mesmerising fountain stood as the labyrinth's beating heart. Its waters danced and shimmered in the dappled sunlight, creating ever-changing patterns that mirrored the labyrinth's complexity.

Surrounding the central plaza, intricately carved stone benches invited weary travellers to pause and reflect. The hushed symphony of rustling leaves and the distant calls of forest birds provided a serene backdrop for moments of contemplation and introspection. Between the stone benches were five doors made of wood that provided entrance to the Labyrinth itself. The doors looked as if they had been grown rather than built - they formed part of the trees growing between the walls surrounding the plaza. It was as though whoever had made this place had wanted to build with the land and trees rather than against it.

Elowen was in awe, her mouth agape and her eyes taking in the wondrous sights. She leaned over to murmur something to Hally, who had been riding next to her, but Hally had stopped, as had all the other entrants. Elowen quickly pulled her horse to a stop, her heart pounding in the realisation that the Tournament was about to begin.

At the front of the party, Buze sat on his horse surveying the central plaza. He turned to face the entrants and said, "It is time. Please dismount."

The entrants all slid from their horses, grabbing their backpacks, and the horses, as if accustomed to this place already, moved to a grassy knoll to the one side of the plaza and began grazing. The entrants moved forward, nervously and silently awaiting their next instructions.

Buze stepped back and gestured behind him, past the fountain to the doors that beckoned to the entrants.

"Each of you will choose a door and proceed to enter the Labyrinth. There will be Locators available to direct you to an exit should you need to leave the Labyrinth. It will bring you back here to safety. I caution you not to use it unless the situation is dire." He paused as he stared around at them, then continued, "Right, choose a door, and let's get this Tournament started."

The entrants all split up and began heading to different doors, their partners following behind with their backpacks and weapons. Gerard and Hant stood before the first door, Jassaly and Kimiad before the second door, Madelyn, Clarissa, and Pollok chose the third door, and Dros and Mol picked the fourth door. That left Damien, Hally, and Elowen to get the fifth and final door.

Buze went around handing out Locators to everyone, which looked like a flat glass disk. Elowen looked at it closely, turning it this way and that, and could make out the outlines of a map of the area they currently stood in. The Locator showed the doors leading from the central plaza, but the rest of the Labyrinth was hidden from view.

Hally tugged on Elowen's arm and directed her toward the last door. Damien followed close behind, throwing his backpack over his shoulder. They stood at the door and then looked back at Buze, awaiting his next instruction. A deathly quiet fell over the plaza as though everything and everyone were holding their breaths.

A shiver passed through Elowen as she felt something move in her pocket. She looked down to see Brannon peek his head out in the form of a small mouse.

Good luck, Mistress. She heard his voice say in her head.

Elowen nodded, swallowing hard against the lump that had formed in her throat. Her heart thumped hard against her chest and she took a deep, calming breath, just as Buze raised his hand and shouted, "Begin!"

Elowen turned to face the door and, grabbing the doorknob, she turned it and heard a click. The door swung inward, opening into darkness and mystery. Elowen glanced at Damien and Hally, who both nodded at her.

"Let's go destroy this Ornette," said Hally and she patted Elowen on the shoulder encouragingly.

They stepped through the door as the other entrants entered their respective doors and the darkness swallowed them whole as the door shut behind them. The only light came from the soft glow emitted by the Locators held by Damien and Elowen. She glanced down at hers to see that they stood in a long passage, the door behind her glowing a soft red colour; the exit to the Labyrinth should they need to take it.

The darkness pressed in on them as they stood there, as though trying to usher them forward. Elowen shivered slightly as the cold clawed at her face and she was grateful for the leather tunic and pants she had put on that morning.

"Time to go," said Hally softly and a small echo answered them. Elowen nodded and began forward, slowly, her feet scuffing the dusty, even ground beneath her leather boots. She put her hands in front of her, and, for what felt like an age, they shuffled along blindly until their hands met the cool, rough wood of another door. Feeling for the handle, Elowen turned and pushed with all her might, until the door inched forward and they were blinded by sudden light entering the passage. They squeezed through the small opening, exiting the claustrophobic passage behind them.

They had entered a huge area where the ancient stone walls of the Labyrinth loomed high above them. The Marasae Labyrinth sprawled before them like a twisted nightmare made real. Its towering walls of ivy-covered stone seemed to shift and breathe as if the very labyrinth itself conspired to confound and entrap those who dared to enter. Elowen, Damien, and Hally stood at the entrance, gazing into the abyss of twisting passages and hidden dangers. The walls were etched with cryptic symbols that seemed to pulse with an eerie, otherworldly light. Elowen glanced at Damien and Hally and was relieved to see determination and excitement etched on their faces, mirroring her own feelings.

"The labyrinth is notorious for its ever-changing passages and mischievous enchantments, so beware and be cautious," said Hally quietly as though not wanting to disturb the silence that pressed in on them. "And don't forget why we are here: to find a way to destroy the Ornette."

Elowen and Damien nodded. At that point, Brannon crept out of Elowen's pocket, transforming into a panther, and he fixed his red eyes on her. *Follow me,* he said to all of them, making them jump. They nodded and reached for the torches that hung on the wall beside the door they had just come through.

The air was thick with a sense of foreboding as they ventured into the maze, their torches casting long, flickering shadows on the cold, moss-covered stones beneath their feet. A faint, ghostly mist clung to the ground, curling around their ankles like an ethereal serpent. The air grew heavy with the scent of damp earth and something more sinister. The ivy-clad walls seemed to close in around them, and the eerie sound of distant whispers echoed through the passages.

"Stay close," Damien muttered, drawing his sword with his free hand, which gleamed in the dim light. "The walls have a way of closing in on you."

Hally clutched her backpack tightly and added, "And watch your step. I've heard of traps hidden beneath the stones."

They moved cautiously, their footsteps echoing through the labyrinth. Each intersection presented a choice, and Brannon guided them. Left, right, left again. He seemed to know exactly where to go without pausing or hesitating.

"This place is like a living nightmare," Damien muttered, his sword at the ready.

Elowen nodded in agreement. "Stay close, both of you."

Brannon paused at the next corner, putting everyone on edge as they paused, too.

"What is it?" whispered Hally.

Listen closely.

Hally moved silently ahead, her keen eyes scanning for traps and hidden dangers. She pressed her ear to the wall and listened intently. "I hear something up ahead," she whispered. "Be on guard."

They all stepped around the corner and were met by a terrifying sight: across from them, in a small open area surrounded by passages, was a Wendigo.

The Wendigo loomed over them, a monstrous creature of ice and despair. Its skeletal frame was draped in tattered, frozen rags, and its eyes burned with a frigid, malevolent light. Its sharp, icicle-like claws extended from its long, bony fingers, ready to rend flesh from bone.

Elowen, Damien, and Hally stood their ground, their determination unshaken. Elowen raised her sword, as did Damien, and both charged forward with a battle cry, their blades slashing through the frigid air. The Wendigo responded with lightning speed, its claws meeting Damien and Elowen's blades with a deafening clash. The creature's strength was otherworldly, and they struggled to keep it at bay.

Hally, nimble as ever, used her agility to dart around the Wendigo, launching a barrage of arrows at its icy form. Some arrows shattered upon impact, but a few found their mark, causing the creature to howl in pain.

Seizing the opportunity, Damien pressed his attack. With a powerful thrust of his sword, he pierced Windigo's heart, and a burst of icy mist erupted from the wound. The creature let out one final, mournful wail before collapsing into a pile of icy shards.

The trio stood panting, their breath visible in the frigid air.

"We did it," Damien said, his voice filled with relief.

Hally retrieved her arrows and nodded. "Quick thinking was all we needed."

Elowen's expression remained solemn as she gazed at the remains of the Wendigo. "But this labyrinth holds more dangers than we can imagine, it seems."

Damien and Hally nodded in agreement, and then, with a shared sense of purpose, they moved deeper into the Marasae Labyrinth, following Brannon closely.

As they ventured deeper into the labyrinth, the walls seemed to close in on them, and the air grew heavy with an eerie stillness. Elowen's torch glowed softly, casting a gentle light that revealed the ancient stonework and the intricate traps hidden within.

"Watch your step," Hally cautioned as she spotted the faint outline of pressure plates on the floor. "The labyrinth is riddled with traps, and some of them are enchanted."

Elowen moved ahead cautiously, her eyes scanning the foundation for any telltale signs of danger. She pointed at a seemingly innocuous tapestry hanging on the wall. "Look there, a hidden glyph. It could be a trigger for something more sinister."

Damien, his sword at the ready, stepped forward to investigate. "We can't just avoid every trigger. Eventually, we'll need to face whatever this labyrinth throws at us."

Elowen nodded in agreement. "We must be vigilant but not overly cautious. We're here for a reason, and the heart of the labyrinth holds our answers."

As they continued their journey, the labyrinth's enchantments grew more insidious. Illusions danced before them, beckoning them down false paths that led to dead ends or worse. Brannon proved invaluable in pointing out these illusions, revealing the proper path forward.

They encountered enchanted statues that wept tears of acid, requiring swift thinking and deft footwork to avoid the deadly droplets. At one point, they stumbled upon a chamber where the walls seemed to come alive, shifting and morphing to block their way. Damien and Elowen's combined strength proved essential in keeping the walls at bay long enough for Hally to find a hidden lever that revealed their escape.

They finally rounded a corner which led them to a small grove of trees, though one tree in the middle was bigger than the rest. It had an inscription carved into its bark that read:

> "Pillar in the sky
> Still as death
> In the peace of thy eye
> The strength of thy breath
> Makes even the heaviest of things fly."

Brannon stepped forward eagerly. *This is it: the entrance to the Tenebris and Passage.*

"Our first riddle," said Damien nervously as he read the inscription.

Elowen clapped her hands together and said, "I get this one. A pillar with an eye and, not breath, but wind, so it must mean a tornado."

There was a pause before they began to make out faint golden lines forming in the bark around the carving. Beginning from the ground and moving upwards, the outline of a door was traced into the wood and it slowly began to fade into visibility. With one final glowing line forming the handle, the wooden door stood awaiting their next move.

Grasping the handle and turning it, Damien pushed the door inwards into what looked like endless blackness. They winced as it made a loud, echoing, scraping noise against the stone floor. Taking a deep breath, Elowen stepped through, followed closely by Hally, Damien, and Brannon, and the door closed noisily behind them.

Elowen moved forward, the torch in her hand barely lighting up the surrounding area as if the darkness had a strength that the light could not penetrate. There was a stifling, claustrophobic feel to the stale air that sent shivers down her spine.

Brannon slipped past them and walked a little way ahead, almost disappearing in the inky blackness. Then he spoke in their minds, making them jump.

We have now entered a place known as Nowhere, which is made up of the Tenebris and Passage. It is not part of Arantaea, but in a different plane of existence completely, so be wary. To our left is the river, Tenebris. Do not fall in, or you will find yourself lost to the Tenebris forever.

Elowen took a cautious step forward. Something stirred in the darkness to her left and she reached for her sword. Damien mimicked her reaction, while Hally reached for her bow and an arrow.

Relax. It is just a Transporter.

Elowen raised her torch higher and gulped as she took in the creature in front of her.

The Transporter was hidden beneath a heavy black cloak, its face barely visible, but it held out one of its hands, which was covered in scabs and bandages.

It requires payment. Brannon looked at Hally expectantly.

Hally reached into the depths of her backpack and withdrew a health potion, which she handed to the Transporter gingerly.

Tell it we require transportation to the Passage, division 60.

Elowen repeated what Brannon had said, her voice sounding strangely muffled as though the darkness were a dampener on sound, too.

The Transporter's hand closed around the bottle of the healing potion and, in a puff of smoke, it disappeared. The Transporter turned to face the front of the boat, waiting for them to join it.

As they stepped carefully into the boat, a hoarse whisper reached their ears.

"Welcome," said the Transporter, "to the Tenebris. Next stop: The Passage, division 60."

Chapter 16

Entering the Passage

They travelled in silence. The only sound was the gentle lapping of the dark water against the sides of the boat. Elowen, Hally, and Damien sat straight-backed and nervous as the Transporter slowly pushed the boat through the river with a long oar. Only Brannon seemed relaxed as he sat curling and uncurling his tail and he stared at Elowen, making her feel even more nervous and uncomfortable.

The boat glided through the inky waters of the river, its lanterns casting feeble rays that barely pushed back the oppressive darkness. Elowen, Damien, and Hally sat close together, their faces illuminated by the flickering light.

"I can't believe we're actually on this river, you guys," said Elowen. "It's so eerie."

Damien nodded, saying, "Yeah, it's like we're sailing through a nightmare. But we had to do this, right? It's the only way to destroy the Ornette."

"I just hope those stories about this River of Eternal Darkness aren't true," said Hally, shivering. "You know, the ones about it leading to the underworld or worse."

"Come on, Hally," said Elowen, bracingly, "You know those are just legends. Superstitions. We're on a quest for knowledge, and sometimes you have to confront your fears."

The boat suddenly jolted, and they all gasped, clutching their seats.

"What was that?" said Damien nervously.

Brannon answered, *Don't you worry. It's just a little turbulence. This river can be tricky, but the Transporter has sailed it a thousand times. We're safe.*

"That's easy for you to say," said Hally, her voice quivering slightly.

Elowen, trying to change the subject, turned to Damien and said, "So, Damien, what did you learn about this river from your research?"

"Well, it's said that the Tenebris is a passage to hidden knowledge. The ancients believed it held the secrets of the universe."

"Secrets of the universe?" repeated Elowen. "That sounds incredible. But how do we find those secrets in this abyss?"

Damien answered, pointing to the water, "It's said that by navigating its twists and turns, we can glimpse the answers to our deepest questions. It's a perilous journey, but we have to trust that it will lead us where we need to go."

"And what if we don't find what we're looking for?" Elowen wondered anxiously. "What if this darkness consumes us?"

"Elowen, we have to believe in our purpose," said Hally firmly. "We're here for a reason, and we have each other to rely on."

Elowen bent over the boat and began trailing her fingers through the pitch-black river that resembled more of a gas than it did water. As she looked down she began to see a face. It was the face of a beautiful woman, smiling prettily up at her. Elowen had the strange urge to get up and jump into the river when Hally suddenly shouted, "What are you doing?!"

Elowen blinked and shook her fuzzy head. She was standing (how that had happened she didn't know), and her foot was on the side of the boat. She quickly sat down and at that exact moment, something exploded out of the still river towards her, its arm outstretched to drag Elowen down into the inky depths. Gone was the pretty woman. Instead, a rotting corpse had taken its place with blue flames for eyes and razor-sharp teeth and claws. It shrieked in fury as both Elowen and

Damien withdrew their swords and Hally drew her bow, and it quickly dove back into the river to escape its imminent death.

Elowen soon became aware of a deafening roar, like that of the wind on a blustery day. They were approaching what looked like an enormous golden crack that glimmered faintly of a thousand lights. The Transporter lifted its arm and began whispering words that Elowen did not understand. The crack began to split wider and Elowen, Damien and Hally had to shield their eyes against the blinding light. As they passed through, the light became unbearably bright and they all shut their eyes. Suddenly, the boat came to a stop, and they became aware that the light, and the deafening roar, had stopped. They opened their eyes and Elowen was the first to let out a gasp of wonder.

Elowen, Hally, Damien, and Brannon were standing in a long, seemingly endless corridor with doors on either side. Elowen gaped as she took in the splendour. It was like they had suddenly been transported to a palace. The corridor was wide and made entirely of marble, with crystal chandeliers and doors that looked like they were made of gold. It was beautiful.

"What do you see?" asked Hally curiously and Elowen noticed they were all staring at her curiously.

"What do you mean?" asked Elowen, confused.

"The passage appears differently to each person who comes here," explained Damien. "I see a corridor like in one of the cheaper hotels of Illfane."

"Really?" said Hally. "I see a forest in the form of a corridor."

Elowen looked at Brannon curiously and he said, *I see a dungeon.*

Elowen's eyebrows rose in consternation. "That could make getting lost quite an easy feat."

Best stick together, then, said Brannon and began moving down the corridor slowly, looking left and right.

Elowen looked to her right and saw that the door had the number 60 on it in swirling writing. She hurried after Brannon, Damien and Hally following close behind.

We are looking for door 68.

Each door was strange in its own way. Some were the size of a mouse hole, others had strange smells coming out of the sides, while others had what looked like blood pooling out of the bottom.

"Where do these doors lead?" asked Elowen curiously.

"Each door leads somewhere completely different," replied Hally. "I once went through a door into a cavernous room that was actually a venomous plant waiting to digest me."

"What?!" cried Elowen. "What did you do?"

"I stabbed the ground with my sword and the room spat me out into the corridor. The point is, don't enter new doors unless you know what lies behind them. We're lucky the Shikari have done endless written studies on the Corridor or we'd be lost."

"Wait," said Elowen suddenly. "How are we meant to leave this place?"

"We use the first door in each division," said Damien, "so door 60 for this division. It'll take us back to an Entrance."

Brannon finally paused as he reached door 68. *This is it, the room that contains the Carver.*

Elowen gulped as she noticed the door smeared with what looked like blood.

It requires a drop of your blood.

"I'll do it," said Hally, and she stepped forward purposefully, but Brannon made a strange sound and pushed in front of her, saying, *It must be the one who wishes to use the Carver.*

Elowen nodded and withdrew her dagger, quickly piercing her palm to draw blood and then smearing it on the door.

The door swung open. They quickly stepped through the door into the room beyond. The room was unlike any other in the realm of

Arantaea. It exuded an aura of enchantment that sent shivers down the spines of Elowen, Hally and Damien. The room was concealed behind a tapestry, woven from threads that shimmered like liquid moonlight. With a gentle tug, the heavy fabric parted to reveal a grand, arched doorway made of polished obsidian. Once through, a soft, lilac-hued glow emanated from the walls, casting an otherworldly light that danced upon the room's marble floor.

At the centre of the chamber stood a circular dais, fashioned from translucent alabaster that seemed to float inches above the ground. Carvings of celestial constellations adorned its edge, and as they approached, they could feel a subtle gravitational pull, drawing them toward the dais like iron to a lodestone.

Above the dais, a vaulted ceiling reached dizzying heights, disappearing into the inky shadows. A massive crystal chandelier, suspended by delicate chains of silver, hung like a frozen waterfall, casting prismatic hues across the room as if the very stars themselves had been captured and tamed.

The walls, adorned with tapestries woven from threads of stardust, depicted scenes from a forgotten age. They depicted brave heroes wielding the Carver, battling dragons, and fending off dark sorcerers in the name of justice and honour. As Elowen gazed upon these enchanting images, she could swear she could hear the clash of swords and feel the rush of magic in the air.

In the centre of the alabaster dais, bathed in an ethereal glow, rested the Carver dagger. Its hilt was a masterpiece of craftsmanship, forged from the finest silver and adorned with sapphires, each gemstone capturing a fragment of the night sky. The blade, however, was the true marvel. Forged from a mysterious metal that gleamed like liquid obsidian, it seemed to drink in the ambient light, creating an ever-shifting dance of shadows across its surface.

The Carver's presence was palpable, a tangible force that hummed with ancient power. Those who dared to approach could feel its call, a siren's song that promised the ability to carve destiny itself. Legends spoke of its ability to cut through not just flesh, but the very fabric of fate, rewriting the stories of those who possessed it.

As Elowen, Damien, and Hally stood in the enchanted chamber, surrounded by the celestial tapestries, bathed in the soft, lilac glow, and gazing upon the Carver, they couldn't help but wonder at the mysteries it held and the adventures it had yet to set in motion. The room itself seemed to hold its breath as if waiting for the next hero to emerge and claim the dagger, their destiny forever altered by its touch.

Elowen reached for the dagger, but Hally placed a hand on her shoulder and gave her a look that seemed to say, "Be careful". Elowen nodded and, slowly, placed one finger upon the hilt. All three of them looked around as though expecting some sort of trap to present itself, but nothing happened. The room remained as it was. Elowen took a deep breath and wrapped her fingers around the hilt, lifting the dagger slightly off the table. It was strangely warm to the touch as if it recognized her touch. Elowen could feel the dagger's power coursing through her veins.

Still, nothing happened. She glanced at Brannon who sat beside her, observing her. And that's when she became aware of a soft whispering that filled the room and in that whisper, she heard a voice, ancient and melodic, speak to her, ever so softly, she might have missed it had there been any other noise in the room.

"Who disturbs my slumber?" the voice whispered, seeming to fill the chamber and Elowen's mind with its presence.

Elowen looked at Brannon and then at Hally and Damien, but they just continued to look at her expectantly. Had they heard the voice, too? Elowen wondered.

"Only my wielder can hear my voice," the voice whispered back as though it had read her mind.

Elowen bit her lip, then said, "I am Elowen Farrowspire. Who are you?"

"I am known by many as the Carver."

Hally and Damien glanced at each other then Hally opened her mouth to ask Elowen who she was talking to, but Brannon hissed and said, *Quiet. She is conversing with the blade.*

The Carver's presence stilled at it seemed to notice the others in the room, and when it spoke again, she saw Damien and Hally jump in fright as though they could hear the voice now, too.

The voice resonated in the very marrow of her bones. "To claim the Carver, you must prove your worthiness," it whispered.

Elowen nodded, steeling herself, and said, "I am ready."

Without warning, the tapestries on the walls came to life, their embroidered scenes writhing and shifting. The heroes depicted in battle seemed to step out of their woven confines, their eyes fixed on Elowen. She understood that the Carver tested its potential wielder's mettle through illusions and memories. Her heart pounded as the heroes advanced, weapons drawn.

With a deep breath, Elowen lifted the Carver. She defended herself with parries and attacks, the Carver feeling like an extension of her arm. Each confrontation felt like a real battle, and sweat beaded on her forehead as she fought off opponents who had never truly lived.

As the battle raged on, the room itself seemed to change. The marble floor beneath her feet shifted and quaked like a tempest-tossed sea. The ceiling descended like a lowering storm cloud, and the walls closed in, threatening to crush her. Elowen's heart raced, her concentration tested to its limits as she battled not only the illusions but the very chamber itself.

She pushed through the trials, her determination unwavering. With every illusion defeated and each obstacle surmounted, the room began to return to its original state. The tapestries stilled, the heroes fading back into their woven stories. Elowen stood in the centre of the chamber, panting but triumphant.

The ancient voice spoke again, filled with approval. "You have proven your worthiness."

The whispering stopped and silence filled the room again. Hally and Damien were watching Elowen carefully from a distance, as though they had moved away from her the moment the trial had started.

"Well, that was dramatic," said Hally, but she smiled and came and patted Elowen on the back. Damien smiled, too, eyeing the Carver cautiously.

"Does that mean we can use it now?" asked Damien, stepping toward Elowen.

Brannon stood up at that moment and stretched lazily, before saying, *Yes, you have proven yourself. You can use it.* Brannon's eyes gleamed as he eyed Elowen expectantly.

Elowen nodded and slowly withdrew the Ornette from beneath her shirt. She bent over, placing it on the stone pedestal in the centre of the room. Lifting the dagger high, she glanced around at Hally, Damien, and Brannon. Then, in one swift movement, she brought the dagger down.

It was as though time slowed and in the time before the dagger could find its mark, the Ornette seemed to reach out its power to caress her thoughts, whispering promises of power and dominion. It was as though it were eager for her to do this, to destroy it, though why, Elowen could not fathom.

The moment the obsidian blade of the Carver touched the necklace, a wave of energy surged through Elowen. She felt as if the very essence of the Carver and the Necklace engaged in an otherworldly battle. The room filled with a blinding, swirling light, casting elongated shadows upon the walls. The air crackled with a cataclysmic aura, and the room quaked as if protesting the impending loss of the necklace's dark power.

The tip of the Carver pierced the Ornette as though it were nothing but a liquid metal. A deafening explosion of darkness erupted, shrouding the entire chamber. Elowen was enveloped in the storm of energy, her very being threatened to be torn asunder by the sheer power of the artefact's destruction. But she held firm, her grip on the Carver unyielding. Slowly, the darkness began to dissipate, vanquished by the dagger's unrelenting will. The remnants of the Ornette crumbled to dust, its malevolence extinguished forever.

Elowen's triumph was short-lived, however. It took her a second to realise that something had gone terribly wrong and to understand why the Ornette had been eager rather than fearful of its destruction.

For in the centre of the room, where Brannon had been seconds earlier, stood a handsome man dressed entirely in black. His jet-black hair cascaded down his shoulders in a tousled and wild manner, reminiscent of the night itself. Each strand seemed to possess an otherworldly sheen, almost as if it absorbed the darkness and secrets of the realm. His hair framed a face that held the essence of an untamed spirit.

But it was his eyes that truly set him apart from all others in Arantaea. Deep, crimson irises gazed out from beneath his inky fringe, a stark contrast to the raven darkness of his hair. These red eyes were windows to his inner power, harbouring an intensity that hinted at hidden magic, both volatile and untamed. They burned with an inner fire, reflecting his passion, determination, and the untold secrets that lay within.

His visage was youthful, yet his eyes bore the weight of countless lifetimes, hinting at an ancient lineage and a destiny intertwined with the very fabric of the world itself. He stood tall and lean, with an agile grace that bespoke an innate skill in combat and a swift, almost ethereal presence.

He smiled at Elowen, his smile not quite reaching his eyes.

"Thank you, Elowen," he said silkily, "for setting me free."

Chapter 17

The Destroyer

Elowen's eyes widened as realisation set in. She glanced at Hally and Damien who were looking shocked and fearful, but both held their swords at the ready, so Elowen raised the Carver to mimic their stances.

"I wouldn't do that if I were you," said Brannon smoothly, smiling slightly. "You were, after all, the one who set me free and, as such, my powers, too."

Elowen looked down at the broken Ornette and back at Brannon. "I may have set you free, but I also set my own powers free, so you should beware, too." Elowen drew herself up, trying to look braver than she felt.

Brannon laughed. "And without any training, you would not know how to use that power. I don't think I have much to fear." He smirked and then said, "But we can always put you to the test."

With a primal cry, Brannon's body underwent a startling transformation. His form blurred and shifted until he emerged as a massive, obsidian-furred black bear. Towering on his hind legs, he unleashed a deafening roar that echoed through the room.

Elowen's eyes widened and she began backing away. She needed to transform, but Brannon had been right; with no training, she had no idea what to do. She nearly screamed as she bumped into Hally and Damien, having forgotten where they were for a second.

"What are you doing, El!" cried Hally. "You need to transform!"

Elowen glanced back at Brannon the Bear and tried to remember what he had done. She searched inside herself for something that might help her transform, but nothing came up. Elowen shook her head frantically.

"He was right," she choked back, fear making her voice waver and break. "I don't know how."

Damien put his hand on her shoulder and said, "It's okay. We'll distract him while you figure it out. Try to remember what you did last time you accidentally transformed."

Then Damien and Hally stepped past Elowen and held up their swords, advancing on the growling bear. Elowen's heart pounded as she realised how much danger her friends were going into and she clutched the Carver tighter, meaning to step forward, too.

"No, El!" shouted Hally. "You need to figure out how to transform. Let us do this."

With that, Hally lunged, swinging her sword toward the bear. Damien followed close behind, swinging his own sword and there was an echoing clang as metal met claws and teeth; Brannon had lunged at the same time to catch the blades between his claws and teeth.

Elowen took a shuddering breath and closed her eyes, reluctantly. What had happened that day in the forest when she had transformed? She thought back, trying hard to ignore the roars and clanging of metal, desperate to open her eyes and watch the battle.

She searched within herself for the answer, for what felt like much too long, until eventually, it came to her. She had been angry, really angry. So Elowen quickly began thinking about the situation they were in and tried to let anger wash over her. She waited for some sign that she was transforming but nothing happened. She continued to stand with her eyes closed.

Panic started to set in. She needed to transform, her friends needed her. As if to prove her point she heard Hally cry out in pain and she wrenched her eyes open to see Hally lying on the floor, a long cut running down her arm as she stared at the approaching Brannon. Her sword lay across the room. Damien tried advancing but got knocked off his feet when Brannon took a swipe at him. Damien's sword clattered to the floor feet away from him.

Brannon began advancing on Hally again.

"No!" screamed Elowen. "Please!" She couldn't let Brannon kill her best friend. She needed to do something. Not caring anymore about transforming, she threw herself toward Brannon, gripping the Carver. She needed to be swift and agile, like a wolf. She raised the Carver as Brannon paused his deathblow to look at her charging toward him. And suddenly, as her eyes met his eyes, she felt something shift in her, and within seconds she was on all fours, the Carver clattering to the ground, and she knew, somehow, she had transformed into a wolf as white as snow.

With the agility of her lupine form, Elowen lunged at Brannon, her powerful jaws snapping dangerously close to his massive bear head. Brannon, his strength magnified in his new form, swiped his enormous paw, and the ground trembled beneath the force of his blow. Elowen agilely dodged.

Their fight was a dance of elemental power. Brannon, in his bear form, possessed immense strength, capable of crushing trees with a single swipe or swatting aside boulders like pebbles. Elowen, as the wolf, was grace personified, her agility and speed making her an elusive target.

Claws met fangs, and the clash of their power sent shockwaves through the room, causing bits of the roof to fall and the earth to shake. They rolled and tumbled across the ground, each gaining the upper hand at different moments. Elowen's teeth grazed Brannon's bear hide, and he retaliated with a deafening roar that sent her reeling.

They circled each other and within seconds, Brannon's form began to shift. His body contorted and expanded, limbs elongating as he transformed into a massive, sleek black panther. His obsidian fur glistened and his predatory red eyes glowed with an unsettling intensity.

Across from him, Elowen felt her lithe body morphing into that of a majestic hawk. Her feathers were white and her talons gleamed like polished emeralds, ready to strike with precision.

With an eerie silence, the battle began again. Brannon, in his panther form, launched himself at Elowen with explosive speed, teeth bared and claws extended. Elowen, in the guise of the hawk, swooped low to avoid Brannon's attack, her wings brushing against his sleek fur. She then ascended gracefully, her sharp talons poised for an aerial assault.

Brannon, undeterred, pivoted and leapt into the air, snapping at Elowen's wing. Their forms blurred and intertwined, a dance of nature's fury and grace. Elowen screeched in pain as her wing was grazed, but her beak struck back with relentless precision, narrowly missing Brannon's red eyes. The hawk circled back, talons slashing at the panther's flank, eliciting a deep growl of pain.

Hally and Damien stood at the edge of the room watching this fight with wide eyes. They dared not try and help for fear of accidentally hitting Elowen as the pair moved so quickly they could barely keep up.

Again, Brannon transformed, this time back into the form of a gigantic bear, and Elowen followed suit with her own transformation; within seconds she was no longer a hawk, but an agile white panther.

Brannon lunged at Elowen, massive paws pounding the forest floor. Elowen dodged and weaved, her purple eyes flashing. She leapt onto the bear's back, claws digging into his fur, but Brannon swiped at her with a powerful paw, sending her tumbling across the room.

Elowen swiftly recovered, her form rippling with an ethereal grace. She melted into the shadows and emerged as a white owl, her wings beating with silence. She dove at Brannon, talons extended, but he roared, causing a wave of primal energy that dispersed her attack.

Elowen soared upward, her form shifting once more, this time into a massive oak tree. Her branches extended, entwining Brannon in a wooden embrace.

Undeterred, Brannon harnessed his own Newidic power, his bear form shimmering with fiery red energies. With a mighty effort, he broke free from Elowen's arboreal grip, branches splintering and falling to the forest floor.

Elowen, her form shifting back into the panther, raced towards Brannon with a renewed determination. She pounced, claws extended, landing a powerful blow on the bear's chest. Brannon staggered backwards, but as Elowen prepared for another strike, he let out a thunderous roar. His own Newidic power surged, manifesting a tempest of red energy that surrounded him in a fiery maelstrom. The flames consumed the panther, but as the fire cleared, Elowen emerged unharmed, her form now a magnificent phoenix, feathers aflame with her own primal magic.

The battle raged on and Damien and Hally watched in awe and fascination as both animals clashed with each other, but something was happening to Elowen: Hally and Damien soon began to notice that Elowen's form kept shifting and changing, not staying solid for more than a few seconds. Elowen suddenly reappeared in her human form and dropped to the earth, colliding with the ground with an uncomfortable crunching sound. Elowen cried out in pain, sweat beading her forehead as she looked up to see Brannon approaching her in his human form. Then he did something she was not expecting: he knelt down beside her and smiled.

"That was a tremendous effort, Elowen. Well done. But I believe you now see why we need to train; not just to learn how to transform, but how to maintain that transformation." He looked across the room to where Hally and Damien were now approaching slowly, their swords raised. "Well, I do believe it's time we said goodbye, my dear Elowen. I'm sure we'll meet again soon." With that, he stood up and bowed to Elowen, before turning to Hally and Damien who had paused their approach.

"Make sure she gets the training she needs," said Brannon softly, dangerously. "When we fight next, I want it to be one for the history books."

Brannon turned on his tail and marched to the door, with Elowen, Hally, and Damien staring after him in surprise.

"You're not going to kill us?" whispered Elowen, her voice raspy and raw as though she had just gotten over a terrible cough.

Brannon paused and, without turning, said, "Not today, Elowen." And with that, he disappeared around the entrance and they heard the door slam shut with finality.

Hally and Damien rushed over to Elowen.

"Are you alright?" asked Damien, holding out his hand to help Elowen off the floor.

She nodded, though cried out as she tried to hold out her hand. "I think I've dislocated my arm."

"Okay, keep it still," directed Damien. " Hally, can you hold her arm and make sure not to move it? I'm going to check it."

He checked for deformities, swelling, and signs of discolouration to ensure no fractures were present, and then he applied gentle traction to the dislocated arm, using a slow, controlled motion to guide the joint back into its proper position. Elowen stared at Damien in surprise.

"How did you know what to do?" Elowen couldn't help but notice how close Damien was and her heart beat loudly enough that it made Elowen uncomfortable.

"I've had plenty of dislocations in the past and many I had to fix myself. You should still not use it too much and try to keep it as still as possible."

Hally grimaced and said, "That looked uncomfortable. Come on you two. We need to get back to the Labyrinth."

"What about Brannon the Destroyer?" asked Elowen nervously.

"We're in no state to take him on again," replied Hally. "I think we take his advice and get you prepared."

"And that means going to the Newids for help," added Damien and Hally nodded.

Elowen sighed and stood up. "Let's go then."

They grabbed their things, Elowen carefully packing away the Carver into her boot, while Hally shouldered the backpack. They made their way to the door, glanced out into the corridor and, upon seeing that it was completely empty, began to head toward room sixty where they would find the exit to the Passage.

They opened door sixty and found themselves along the edge of the Tenebris. Before them stood another Transporter and they quickly took their positions in the boat.

"Please transport us to the Marasae Labyrinth," said Hally clearly, and they all grabbed the boat as it jerked into motion.

The trip back felt quicker than their first trip on the Tenebris, and it wasn't too long before the Transporter pulled his boat up to the edge and let them disembark. They headed to the nearest door and pushed it open, the light from the Labyrinth blinding the three companions momentarily. They hurried through the door, shut it, and nearly jumped out of their skins when a voice said, "What took you so long?"

Lord Gimrad, stood in the shade of a nearby tree, arms crossed, looking concerned and a little annoyed.

"I've been here for an hour waiting for you three," he continued, starting toward them. He looked at Elowen and said, "Did you do it?"

Elowen nodded, grasping the remnants of the Ornette and lifting it to show Lord Gimrad.

"We ran into a bit of a problem, though," she started, then stopped when she felt Hally nudge her arm.

"What do you mean?" asked Lord Gimrad softly.

Hally stepped forward and laughed, saying, "She means she dislocated her arm. Nothing else. But we managed to fix it, didn't we, Damien?"

Damien nodded and Elowen frowned but kept quiet. She had been meaning to share the news about Brannon the Destroyer escaping, but perhaps Hally had a good reason for not wanting to share it.

"Are we still in time to complete the tournament?" Damien asked quickly and Master Gimrad nodded slowly.

"Most of the other champions have made it out by now," said Lord Gimrad, and he took another step toward them.

"Great, then we still have a chance," said Elowen slowly.

Lord Gimrad smiled then, and said, "I think not, Elowen."

Suddenly, arrows whizzed through the air, and enchanted ropes dropped from the branches above, ensnaring the trio. In a matter of moments, Elowen, Damien, and Hally found themselves bound and surrounded by a group of Shikari.

"What is going on?" yelled Damien, pulling against his restraints.

Lord Gimrad spoke then, and as he spoke, the rest of the entrants stepped out of the shadows and came closer to where the trio were standing.

"These three have been caught trying to help the Newids, our enemy, by assisting Elowen here to become a formidable weapon, just like Brannon the Destroyer of old. They planned to help the other Newids escape, too." he gestured behind him and out stepped the other captured Newids, bound by enchanted ropes and being pulled along by more Shikari.

"That's a lie," shouted Damien and Hally and Elowen nodded vigorously. "Father, please, you know that's not true."

But Master Gimrad ignored his son and turned to the rest of the listening Shikari. "We cannot let the Newids destroy our precious guild. The Shikari are stronger and more powerful and we will make an example of these Newids, starting with that one." He pointed at Elowen and Elowen's heart began to pound. "Tie them all together!"

The other Newids were brought forward and shoved into Damien, Hally and Elowen.

"What is going on?" whispered Elowen and Hally shook her head.

"You still have the Carver in your boot, right?" said Hally and Elowen nodded. "Right, I'm going to cut you loose and you need to run! Got it?" Hally reached into Elowen's boot and surreptitiously brought out the Carver. Hally discreetly began to saw through the ropes that bound their hands, using the Carver which could cut through enchanted things. She kept her actions concealed beneath her cloak and used every bit of her skills to ensure the Shikari remained unaware of her actions.

Eventually, Elowen felt the ropes loosen and she moved her arms slowly to get the feeling back into them. She should run, she knew, but her heart screamed at her to stay and help the others. Elowen realised that a more direct approach was necessary to distract the captors and buy them the time they needed to escape. She discreetly whispered to Damien and Hally to be prepared for her signal. Hally looked ready to argue, but, with a deep breath, Elowen closed her eyes, and her hands began to glow with an ethereal light. She focused on a creature, a majestic forest owl with pristine white feathers. As she channelled her powers, her body started to shimmer and morph. Within moments, Elowen had transformed into the very owl she had envisioned, with white feathers and piercing purple eyes.

Elowen took flight and was relieved when her transformation had the desired effect: The Shikari began shouting, pointing at her owl form, completely distracted from Hally helping the others escape. Within seconds, the other Newids had been released too and they each transformed into massive wolves, growling at the Shikari.

"What is happening!" yelled Master Gimrad. "Those were enchanted ropes! Who set them free?"

"I did!" yelled Hally, as she, at last, finished freeing everyone. She raised the Carver, while Damien grabbed his sword and the wolves all growled from their positions. Elowen swooped down and landed beside the door to the Tenebris and transformed back into her usual form.

"Come on!" she yelled, and opened the door, revealing the black nothingness again. Before the Shikari could even think of responding, they all piled through and shut the door behind them.

Then they ran to the nearest boat, piling in quickly.

"Go! Go!" they all yelled.

"Take us to the Newids!" shouted Hally.

"Take us to Rostefen!" said Freya, Tern and Jim clearly, Freya quickly passing a small potion into the hands of the Transporter.

The boat began to move, just as the door behind them opened and the Shikari began piling through, Master Gimrad in the front.

Master Gimrad scowled as he saw them getting away and he yelled one final parting promise, "I will find you, Elowen Farrrowspire, and I will kill you myself!"

Chapter 18

The Escape

Soon, the Shikari disappeared in the darkness of the Tenebris and Elowen breathed a sigh of relief. They had escaped, somehow. She could barely believe it. Her hands shook and she glanced around at the other occupants of the boat. Freya, Tern and Jim were conversing in soft undertones while Damien stared at the sword in his hand, his face white and shock written all over it. Hally was still staring at where the Shikari had disappeared.

Hally, still a bit on edge from the escape, took a deep breath and turned to her companions. "Well, that was a close call," she said, her voice laced with tension. "I can't believe we managed to escape."

Damien took a breath and said, "What just happened? I thought they were meant to help us. We are, technically, Shikari now, after all."

Freya shook her head and spoke up, "You will be considered lost to the Shikari now that you have left the Shikari to come with us."

"But we had no choice," muttered Elowen. "They were going to kill us."

"I still don't get it," cried Damien, throwing his hands in the air. "We did everything my father told us to do."

Freya smiled sadly and replied, "They needed someone to blame and you were the perfect scapegoat."

"Blame for what?"

Freya glanced at Tern and Jim and then said, "Well, while you were in the labyrinth, the Newids of Rostefen attacked Pamor Tower in an effort to save us."

Elowen clapped her hand to her mouth in shock and dismay. "What happened?"

"Well, the Newids conducted extensive reconnaissance, using their shapeshifting abilities to blend in with the surrounding environment and observe the layout of Pamor Tower. They transformed into various creatures, such as birds and rodents, to infiltrate the tower unnoticed. Then they coordinated an attack on Pamor Tower. Some of them took on the forms of powerful jaguars to create diversions outside the tower. Their aim was to draw the attention of the tower's defenders and keep them occupied while the rescue mission took place inside. Within the tower, the shapeshifters changed forms strategically, confusing and disorienting the guards...."

"All this to rescue you?" Damien said, stunned.

"Yes, but, unfortunately, we had already been moved. Your father took it upon himself to have us taken via a secret tunnel out of the Tower."

"But what does that have to do with us?" whispered Hally, confused.

"Master Gimrad seemed to connect all their prior knowledge of Pamor Tower to you," Freya said, looking at Elowen. "He needed someone to blame and, as you are half Newid, you were the perfect person to pin this on."

"And, what?" said Hally suddenly. "We were collateral damage?"

"Yes," replied Freya. "I'm truly sorry this happened to you."

Silence followed her words as they thought all this through. Elowen was stunned and a little nervous.

"What now," Elowen asked, biting her lip.

"Now we go to Rostefen," said Freya slowly as though this were obvious.

The boat began to slow and soon pulled up alongside the walkway where a door was located. Freya, Jim and Tern hopped out of the boat and Elowen, Hally and Damien followed, more slowly and warily.

Freya led the way to the door and stood waiting for the rest of the party to join her. A sense of anticipation and wonder filled Elowen's heart as she stepped up to the door, reaching for the handle.

The door seemed to emanate a soft, ethereal glow, and its ornate carvings depict intricate patterns of vines and leaves. The knob felt cool and inviting to the touch, and as Elowen turned it, the door swung open with a whisper of enchantment.

Stepping through the doorway, Elowen was immediately enveloped in a breathtaking transformation. The world on the other side was unlike anything she had ever seen before. She found herself standing at the edge of a lush and vibrant forest, but this was no ordinary woodland. It was as though Nature herself had woven a tapestry of enchantment and magic into every aspect of this place.

The air was filled with the sweet aroma of wildflowers and earthy moss. Sunlight filtered through the emerald canopy above, casting dappled patterns on the forest floor. The trees stood tall and wise, their trunks adorned with intricate carvings and glowing, luminescent moss. She could hear the soft whispers of leaves and the melodic chirping of birds that seemed to harmonise with the gentle rustling of the leaves.

As the party took their first steps deeper into the forest, they noticed that the path beneath their feet was not made of ordinary earth, but rather a shimmering, silver-tinged moss that cushioned each step and seemed to respond to their presence. Small, iridescent creatures flitted about, leaving trails of sparkling dust in their wake.

Further into the forest, they came across a babbling brook with water so clear that it appeared to be liquid crystal. The sound of the water was soothing, and Elowen dipped her fingers in, feeling a surge of rejuvenating energy flow through her body.

Magical flowers of every colour imaginable lined the path, their petals radiating a soft, gentle glow. Hally reached out to touch one, and it shimmered and swayed in response, releasing a sweet, otherworldly scent into the air. The forest seemed to be alive with the hum of hidden wonders and secrets.

They kept walking for what felt like an age and every now and then a jaguar would lope out of the forest and join them, until about twenty jaguars had joined their party.

They followed Freya, Tern and Jim on a windy route through the trees until Elowen felt quite lost. As they journeyed deeper into the forest, the world around them continued to dazzle with its enchanting beauty. Birds with jewel-toned feathers serenaded them from the treetops, and shafts of sunlight filtered through the canopy, casting shifting patterns of light and shadow upon the forest floor. The air was scented with the sweet aroma of wildflowers, and a gentle breeze played with their hair.

The sun began to drop below the trees. As the forest path led them onward, it began to widen and open up, revealing a captivating sight ahead. Emerging from the dense foliage, they caught their first glimpse of Rostefen, the fabled forest city. Nestled among the ancient trees, the city was a marvel of Newid architecture, its buildings constructed from the living wood of the forest itself. Towering treehouses interconnected by winding bridges loomed overhead, blending seamlessly with the natural surroundings.

As they entered Rostefen, they were greeted by the melodious hum of Newidian songs and the laughter of forest dwellers going about their daily lives. The buildings were adorned with intricate carvings and luminescent moss that cast a soft, gentle glow. Newid children played among the branches, and market stalls overflowed with exotic fruits and magical trinkets.

The heart of Rostefen was a massive, ancient tree known as the Mothertree, which served as the spiritual and communal centre of the city. The Mothertree was massive, with its gnarled branches stretching high into the sky, providing both shelter and a focal point for the Newid community. It was rumoured to be as old as time itself and was believed to possess a deep connection to the magic that enabled the Newids to shift forms.

Elowen marvelled at the architecture of Rostefen which was a harmonious blend of nature and artistry. The buildings were constructed from organic materials, seamlessly integrated into the forest's flora, often covered with moss and ivy that helped them blend in with the surrounding environment. Bridges and walkways made from intertwined branches and vines connect the different parts of the city, allowing the Newids to traverse the treetops with ease.

The city hummed with an energy that echoed the cycle of life within the forest. Luminous, bioluminescent plants and glowing crystals illuminated the city at night, casting an enchanting and magical glow. The air was scented with the perfume of blooming flowers, and the sound of rustling leaves and bird songs wove a serene melody throughout the city.

Elowen stood gobsmacked as she took in the sights around her and she knew that Damien and Hally were doing the same beside her. She was hardly aware that Freya, Tern and Jim had moved ahead and were speaking to someone. Elowen thought she heard her name mentioned and she quickly looked toward Freya, who was talking to a man with snow-white hair, not unlike Elowen's hair. He wore what looked like a robe made of finely woven, luxurious fabric in earthy tones. The fabric itself was adorned with intricate patterns that mimic the textures of bark, leaves, or even feathers, symbolising his deep connection to nature. He wore a crown made of interwoven vines and leaves, adorned with precious stones and gems that glisten like dewdrops. The man's brown eyes found Elowen's and he smiled warmly at her.

"Elowen, my dearest daughter." The man opened his arms wide toward Elowen.

"Father?" Elowen whispered, her voice catching slightly.

The man nodded and Elowen found herself running into his arms. He was tall, taller than Elowen, and he hugged her tightly.

"I'm so sorry, my dear girl," he whispered into her ear. "For everything you have gone through to get here and that I was not there to help with any of it."

Tears slipped from Elowen's eyes and she buried her face in his robe for a second before pulling away to look into his kind face.

"I want you to know," he continued, "that you and your friends are welcome here."

"We are?" Elowen whispered, surprised.

"Would you like that?"

"Yes!"

"Then you will stay here," he said firmly, loudly, and Elowen noticed then that a whole crowd of Newids had surrounded their party. They all began muttering to themselves and one Newid with brown hair and brown eyes stepped forward.

"But they are human."

Freya stepped forward and told them about how these humans had saved her, Tern and Jim. This sparked more muttering and though some seemed unimpressed, a few had more welcoming looks on their faces. Then Elowen's father put up his hands and all fell silent.

"My daughter is not human. She is one of us."

"Prove it!" shouted some of the Newids.

Elowen blanched. Her heart began hammering and she had to take a deep breath to steady herself. She looked around at the expectant faces surrounding her and bit her lip. She hoped she would be able to impress - it seemed everything rested on her shoulders now.

Elowen stood at the centre of the clearing and the moonlight filtered through the dense canopy above, casting an ethereal glow on the Newids.

Elowen closed her eyes and took a deep breath. The atmosphere around her seemed to quiver with an otherworldly energy. A subtle ripple passed through the air, and her form started to change.

At first, her figure blurred, like an artist smudging the lines of a masterpiece. Then, in a mesmerising display of fluidity, Elowen transformed. Her body twisted and contorted, reshaping itself with an uncanny grace. She became a sleek, white-coloured panther, her fur glistening with an otherworldly sheen. The Newids gasped in awe as they witnessed the seamless transition from human to feline.

The panther prowled gracefully around the clearing, its movements embodying a combination of feral power and innate elegance. Elowen, in her new form, exuded an aura of primal strength.

But she wasn't finished yet.

With another concentrated effort, the panther dissolved back into the form of Elowen. This time, however, she chose a more fantastical guise. Her skin took on an iridescent, ethereal glow, and her hair transformed into shimmering strands of moonlight. Elowen's eyes sparkled like stars, and a pair of translucent wings unfurled from her back. She hovered above the ground, radiating a celestial presence that left her fellow Newids in silent admiration.

The onlookers erupted into cheers and applause. She smiled, her eyes gleaming with satisfaction, knowing that she had not only impressed her peers but had also left an indelible mark on their memories. The clearing echoed with the whispers of awe.

Elowen's father stared at her with pride and he smiled at the surrounding Newids.

"My daughter is a Newid with many forms. Now do you consent to having her and her friends stay?"

There was more muttering and eventually a Newid stepped forward and said, "Yes, she may stay. But she will need to attend the Newid School to perfect her transformations, Lord Farrowspire."

Elowen's father nodded and turned thoughtfully to Elowen. "You have come at the right time, Elowen. There will be an induction of our newest Newid students into our school. You can join them.

Elowen nodded. "Thank you. It would be my honour."

Lord Farrowspire smiled and said, "Come, let me take you to your rooms that you can use until you leave for school."

Elowen's father guided them through the suspended bridges and tree-lined pathways towards their individual rooms.

Elowen's room, nestled high among the branches, was a spacious and elegantly crafted treehouse with large, arched windows that framed breathtaking views of the surrounding forest. The walls were adorned with intricate tapestries woven from leaves and vines, depicting scenes of nature's beauty. A comfortable, canopied bed made from woven vines and adorned with soft moss awaited Elowen, providing a cosy and natural place to rest. Luminescent mushrooms served as delicate and warm lighting, casting a soft glow that enhanced the room's ethereal atmosphere. A small balcony opened to the outside, allowing Elowen to immerse herself in the sounds of the forest.

Hally's room was situated in a massive hollowed-out tree trunk, its entrance veiled by cascading vines. The interior was illuminated by the gentle glow of fireflies, creating a serene and calming ambience. Hally's bed, fashioned from the bark of ancient trees, was surrounded by shelves adorned with crystalline formations and delicate sculptures carved from driftwood. A natural spring, redirected through the roots, provided a refreshing and soothing water feature within the room. The air was scented with the fragrance of blooming flowers, adding a touch of the outdoors to the cosy dwelling.

Damien's room, located on the outskirts of the city, offered a blend of the organic and the artistic. The walls were covered in murals depicting the various forms of wildlife found in the forest, showcasing the Newids' connection to the natural world. Damien's bed, fashioned from intertwined vines and adorned with vibrant moss, was accompanied by a desk carved from a single, ancient tree stump. Soft, multicoloured foliage served as a natural canopy, diffusing the sunlight that filtered through the branches.

All three rooms were located close to each other and when Elowen's father left, Damien and Hally quickly made their way to Elowen's room and sat upon the cosy, moss-covered couches that lined the one wall.

Hally was the first to speak and she smiled as she said, "We actually made it! We're finally in Rostefen. No humans have ever made it here!" She looked at Damien and grinned.

"I hope they will let us come with you to this school," said Damien wistfully. "It would be amazing to be able to witness Newids at work."

Elowen nodded and said, "I hope so, too. I don't want to go alone." She sighed. "I still can't believe what happened with your father and the other Shikari."

Damien nodded. "Me neither. But we'll be safe here. No human has ever ventured into Newidian territory."

"Plus we'll be moving to the school soon," said Hally. "That will make it even more difficult to find us."

Elowen nodded and made her way over to the window overlooking the city. As the golden hues of the setting sun bathed Rostefen in a warm embrace, Elowen stood on the highest platform, gazing out over the sprawling forest city. The air was filled with the gentle rustle of leaves and the melodic symphony of the creatures that called the woodland home.

Below, the intricate architecture of the city merged seamlessly with the ancient trees, the result of a shared vision between the Newids and the natural world. The suspended bridges and treehouses stood as a testament to the harmonious coexistence that had flourished.

A gentle breeze played with Elowen's hair, and a sense of fulfilment settled in her heart. The challenges that had once seemed insurmountable had become stepping stones, paving the way for a brighter future for her.

The sun dipped below the horizon, casting a cascade of colours across the sky. Stars emerged, twinkling like diamonds in the velvet night.

In that moment, Elowen felt a profound connection to the forest, to Rostefen, and to her shapeshifting abilities. Elowen Farrowspire smiled, knowing that she had finally made it home.

Elowen will return in the next adventure of the Farrowspire Chronicles.